RED BRANCH COMMAND

A RED BRANCH MISSION

BOOK 3

BLAZE WARD

KNOTTED ROAD PRESS

Red Branch Command
A Red Branch Mission: 3
Blaze Ward
Copyright © 2025 Blaze Ward
All rights reserved
Published by Knotted Road Press
www.KnottedRoadPress.com

ISBN: 978-1-64470-457-8

Cover Art: GetCovers.com

Cover and interior design copyright © 2025 Knotted Road Press

Reviews
It's true. Reviews help. Even a short one, such as, "Loved it!" So please consider reviewing this book (and all of the ones you've read) on your favorite retailer site.

Never miss a release!
If you'd like to be notified of new releases, sign up for my newsletter.

http://www.blazeward.com/newsletter/

Buy More!
Did you know that you can buy directly from the Knotted Road Press website?

https://www.knottedroadpress.com/shop/

CONTENTS

ALSO BY BLAZE WARD

The Hunter Bureau

Start with: Mirrors

Fairchild

Start with: Fairchild

Last Stand

Start with: Lost Dreams

The Lazarus Alliance

Start with: Escape

Shadow of the Dominion

Start with: Longshot Hypothesis

Star Dragon

Start with: Birth of the Star Dragon

Kincaide's War

Start with: The Eden Package

Star Tribes

Start with: Winterstar

Blaze also writes Action-Adventure Here

ESSAY: RED BRANCH
COMMAND

When I was in high school in the mid-1980s, I noticed that all US history functionally stopped in 1945, basically with the end of World War Two. Forty years of gap, where you might hear that there was a war in Korea and maybe something about a place called Vietnam, but almost nothing was taught about it. Or the Civil Rights Movements from Brown vs. BOE Topeka forward.

Odd, that.

One of my High School history teachers, however, served in Vietnam, and had turned into a raging Red by the time I met him nearly twenty years later. He had a radically different view on a lot of things than the usual football coach who taught history classes. (Most of them were republican in that day. Probably still are, and much worse.)

I did learn a bit more than the average bear. Later, I got undergraduate degrees in political science (emph: International Politics) and philosophy (emph: Epistemology) and did my Masters work in International Political Economics at Claremont under a guy who got his PhD in Tel Aviv and liked to talk about how an AK-47 with a folding stock would fit in a briefcase, because that was how he carried his during the 1967 War while he was in grad school. I also studied under Nathaniel Davis, a former US Ambassador and Eisenhower's Soviet Desk Officer.

Learned a lot. Not enough, but I like to learn. To study. Writing the Red Branch novels has involved diving deep into things that hardly get any mention. And what is covered is usually at least half American propaganda.

But I have fun digging. And I need to apologize to one of my first readers, who volunteered to read books 2-4. He's Finnish. Knew that. Didn't know at the time that he was Karelian, and that his grandfather had had to pack up the entire family and move them to Helsinki from what eventually ended up being Russian territory after the Winter War invasion. Whole different take on a lot of things from the standard US one, and he loves these books, once he got over hating every single one of the characters and the concept, mostly because they were all Soviets. My fault, but at least I entertained him.

Sasha is Ukrainian. So is Gennadi. That's intentional on my part, when writing in 2024. The Ukrainians were some of the toughest, meanest, baddest elements of the Soviet Army that defeated Hitler, but the Russians have turned into a third world banana republic these days. Or, as my friend J* says, 'Russia is a gas station with a foreign policy.'

My goal with every Red Branch book is to keep things as close to historically accurate as I can. What might have happened. What did happen. Who was there.

Previously, I mentioned never wanting "real" people in any of these books. I decided to make an exception with Red Branch Command because I wanted them in Southern California for the action, instead of Europe or South America.

There's a dude who lived and worked in SoCal Aviation. If

you know planes, you know Kelly Johnson. Everything I've read about the man kinda frightens me, because he was a literal genius at an instinctive level when it came to aeronautics.

There's a story that someone showed him a rough sketch and asked about efficiency. Off the cuff, he replied that it would be a little under twenty percent. Months later, after extensive calculations were run by hand, the number was something like 18.5%. Kelly just looked at it and knew the answer off the top of his head.

He was amazing. Not necessarily all that great as a person, depending on who you ask, but knew his shit. I wanted him to meet Lyuba. I wanted those two to come up with something entirely new. Circling back, yet again, to the Blackhawk comics, because it starts there.

Originally, the Blackhawks during WW2 flew a variant of the Grumman XF5F Skyrocket in the comics. The aircraft itself never really worked out, but was utterly distinct visually, so the folks doing the comic took it and ran.

Later, when the comics hit the 1950s, the team upgraded to the Lockheed XF-90. That jet was a failed experiment, but that was because Kelly built it extra rugged and heavy, at a time when nobody really knew what to expect at transsonic and supersonic speeds.

On top of that, the two Westinghouse J34-WE-11 axial-flow turbojet engines were underpowered and unreliable. (A nice way of saying utter crap.) Plus, the whole concept of the penetration fighter as the US Air Force envisioned it in the late 1940s got shelved.

But I wanted that callback. The F-90B that the original Blackhawks flew in the comics from 1950-57. Designed by that same Kelly Johnson. What if you could put better engines in and make it lighter for production? And maybe only needed to ever build a small number of them for expert pilots, so you could push the envelope a little in performance and operations?

So you will have Kelly, Sasha, and Lyuba sitting at a table in the commissary, inventing a different future from the one that actually unfolded.

More interestingly, as Silver Eagle focused on Lyuba, I wanted this novel to spotlight Gennadi. The man who built the team and continues to be that shadowy figure behind the scenes, conning the Brits into thinking he's a White Russian. They were not the most effective at espionage in those days, when it came to fighting the Soviets. (As the saying goes, not even the sharpest *spoons* in the drawer.)

But the Brits had fantastic designs. And the bleeding edge jet engines. If they'd had money, they would have built stuff the USAF would have been jealous about, instead of the other way around, because they were in the process of losing the empire that had funded everything, but not yet come to grips with penury.

Gennadi, however, is GRU. Soviet Military Intelligence. And a deep-cover operation so carefully buried that even the MGB doesn't know. (MBD evolves into KGB in another couple of years, but I try to be historically accurate when the information is available.)

The MGB thinks he's a White, so they decide that the Red Branch must be destroyed. That causes them to activate kill teams made of of LA bikers.

I don't know how accurate some of that was, but it fits perfectly well with what I have learned about the sorts of behind-the-lines, undercover units that infested most of the Western European nations that became NATO in this period. And I did base them on some of the actual biker gangs that existed in those days, generally made up of men who had fought in the war, and had such terrible PTSD that they could not return to the lives they had prior. (We are generally better at understanding, even if the DoD still does a lousy job treating it. Just ask any of my vet friends who have gotten out in the last decade.)

Soviet on Soviet war. On an LA Freeway. And Gennadi's time in the spotlight, because he was a top fighter pilot as recently as four years ago, before the crash that nearly killed him.

But, like the others, circumstances will drive him to rise. And to recover himself somewhat, as he continues in the role of something like M from the Bond books. The commander of the base operations, because it takes mechanics to repair and maintain aircraft.

Jets get old and surly, and things need to be replaced after a certain number of hours. Everything needs a ground crew to keep it tuned and flying. In the Red Branch books, those folks are generally nameless and mostly faceless so that I don't have to track them with any great detail. They are also frequently Irish Reds. Anti-British to the core and Anti-colonial, but generally neutral and would appreciate it if the British got the fuck out and stayed out so they could live their own lives without interference.

Most of Ireland got its freedom in the 1920s, but Northern Ireland has always been something of an English colony in makeup. And The Troubles will be getting nasty in a few more years, as the IRA and all the various elements of Irish nationalism started getting assistance from Communist governments seeking to tear down the West. Future books might touch on this, but I honestly can't see Sasha and Gennadi staying at this for another decade. Or rather, maybe

Sasha becomes Red Branch Command himself and Gennadi retires.

I don't know. Don't have to know. It is 1949 and there are a lot of things still in the future that might come up later, depending on how it all shakes out. Malaya and Kenya and India and Vietnam and a bunch of other places would like to throw off the chains of colonialism, or are in the process. The CIA spent most of the 40s and 50s overthrowing any government that looked at the US with even a hint of side-eye. (Go look up Guatemalan history in the 20th Century, but you won't like what you find.)

It's a mess, and I'm not going to sugarcoat the actual history under a thick layer of pseudo-patriotism. That's why my Finnish buddy is willing to read them, because it's honest. The Soviets did terrible things, but so did the Nazis and the Americans. Winners write the history books. And I still believe that the world is far better off today than it ever would have been had Hitler, Stalin, or Khrushchev been successful at their world-dominating goals.

Red Branch Command, then, becomes the transition point away from just fighting comic-book villains in the Werewolf Legion and starts looking at the evolving Cold War, which is still being born in 1949.

Churchill gave the Iron Curtain speech, the "Sinews of Peace" address, on 5 March 1946, at Westminster College in Fulton, Missouri, when he was in the Opposition, having lost the 1945 election that saw Clement Attlee installed as Prime Minister, before himself returning to power in 1951. Attlee really did sell Stalin jet designs that became critical to the beginnings of this series.

The Berlin Blockade by Soviet/East German forces started on 24 June 1948 and ran until 12 May 1949, nearly a year, with the US Air Force and friends flying an impossible number of transports in constantly, in order to keep West Berlin fed and operational. How it never started the next world war, I still don't know after reading several books on the subject, but I suspect that the East Germans were bluffing and Stalin refused to back them up when the US called them on it.

The world is becoming divided into East and West, with the North/South split (the so-called Third World) only starting to take shape as anti-imperialism sees overseas colonies finally breaking free. This shows up in Red Branch 4, The Free City, because Tito was an early proponent of the Third World Neutrality movement.

So you have messy. And it gets worse, but first, Soviet bureaucrats decide that the Red Branch must be destroyed. So they will call out all stops to do it.

AIRCRAFT RESEARCH: THE NIGHTOWL (F-90B)

Kelly Johnson designed the XF-90 for the US Air Force Penetration Fighter program, intended to accompany American bombers deep into Soviet airspace to run interference by engaging defensive aircraft before the bombs fell. This was before ICBMs. It was even before the MGM-1 Matador Surface-to-Surface short-range nuclear-armed cruise missile became operational (1952+).

Kelly and his people designed some amazing aircraft at Lockheed, including the P-38. Later, they would design and build the U-2 and the SR-71 Blackbird. The generation after Kelly retired went on to create the F-117 Stealth fighter that was able to slip into Iraq without being seen on radar, in order to bomb key command and control facilities.

Kelly had a shop now famously known as The Skunk Works. Other aircraft manufacturers have similar things, but nobody has done as much in the field of aviation.

As mentioned above, the Penetrating Fighter Program was originally a project to develop a long-range, high-speed, air superiority jet fighter that could accompany American bombers deep into Soviet territory from bases in West

Germany, Britain, or Turkey, among others. You need a lot of range. And a lot of speed.

At the same time, some nitwit somewhere got the idea that American fighters no longer needed guns, and should instead pack salvos of unguided short-range rockets. The logic, near as I can understand, was that American defenders would fly right up to a Soviet bomber and shoot it with the equivalent of a shotgun. And they spent several years trying to get it to work, thought they never did.

Eventually, (self-)guided missiles will become sophisticated to work, but Sidewinder and the others are still several years in the future and don't really become effective and introduced into service in 1956 with the US Navy.

However, if you are penetrating Soviet airspace as an escort, you need to kill enemy fighters. And that's going to mean dogfighting with them in 1950. Shoot them full of holes so they explode or crash. Can't do that well with unguided rockets.

Worse, the F-86 Sabre started out with six .50 caliber (12.7mm) machine guns, when everyone else was upgrading to 20mm or even 30mm (the Brits moved there first I think). 30mm is a thin-shelled munition filled with explosives. .50 ball might penetrate. Might bounce off.

For the comics, the Blackhawks in the 50s flew the F-90, but I wanted it ground it in something both more effective and more realistic, which was why Kelly appears in this and the following novel, before fading off. The Brits had fantastic jets (and no money to exploit them), so I had Gennadi work out a deal for Sapphires. And Kelly take the original XF-90 design and make it one hell of a lot lighter in (limited) production under a special contract with the CIA (you'll see when you get deeper).

Most importantly, I read a note about how they also thought in 1950 that a single pilot would be able to fly, navigate, watch various gauges, and use a radar system to track enemy jets.

Uhm, information overload, anyone? You need a second set of eyes in a night-fighter.

In my research, Lockheed was also building what would become the F-94, a first-generation jet powered all-weather day/night interceptor aircraft with a two-man crew, because one was supposed to operate the radar. That fit with my two-person teams, so I had Kelly take an F-94 bow and mate it to the fuselage and rear of a XF-90 with Sapphires and 30mm British cannons, in order to make what the Blackhawk comics might have called the F-90B/C, but I simply called it Strix, after the malevolent a bird of ill omen from Greek antiquity.

After all, it is a night-fighter, though sometime in this time frame they start calling them All-Weather Fighters instead. But if you have expert pilots already, and Kelly's willing to push the envelope a little with two expert test pilots offering suggestions from the Nightviper and the Sabre, we can improve the Strix into a top-notch, front-line, all-everything fighter, which is exactly the sort of thing that nobody was wanting to build in 1950, and everybody has been trying to accomplish since at least 1990.

The only thing it doesn't do it carriers, because navalizing a jet adds a lot of weight. Don't think I haven't thought about it. Imagine Red Branch Command becoming an Admiral. (Heh) Because why the hell not? And I might. This series keeps filling me with new ideas. And technology keeps moving forward, with some radical new revolution in jet aviation seemingly happening every year from 1943 through at least 1955.

Possibly more, but I've kind of cut off my research there for now. In 1956, the Brits will functionally shut down most aviation research and collapse all those fantastic companies down into a handful of survivors by about 1960. Khrushchev will come to power in 1953, and cut Soviet Aviation to the bone in about the same timeline as he bets heavily on nuclear missiles and eventually ICBMs. The Soviets will still make some fantastic jets, with MiG-15, -17, and -19, as well as entries from Sukhoi, Tupolev, and Yakovlev.

The Americans will counter with the fantastic Century Series of jets. There are all sorts of adventures coming for the Red Branch, as I've really only just started.

For now, come take a ride on a twin-jet interceptor.

Shade and sweet water

blaze

West of the Mountains, WA

April 2025

PART ONE
IRELAND

CHAPTER 1

Comrade General Zinoviy Shuysky put down the file he had been reading, pausing to light a cigarette and suck down a lungful of acrid, heavy smoke before he picked up the newspaper sitting next to it on his desk.

The Red Branch had not been his idea, but he had shepherded it into existence, locating Comrade Colonel Gennadi Nazarenko to handle operations and recruiting, then providing the man the cover and resources to accomplish his task.

The GRU, the Soviet Armed Forces Main Intelligence Directorate, was concerned with a vast array of issues worldwide. China about to finally fall to Comrade Mao's armies. The impending and ongoing dissolution of the British Empire, even as the French and the others joined them, everyone watching their particular sun set.

Perhaps one third of all the Nazi scientists alive at the end of the war had ended up prisoners of the Soviet Union. Another third were American guests, but Zinoviy understood that few of those men were working penance in labor camps. The other third had escaped but were being sought. Especially a few in South America.

A great many war criminals had also been rounded up. A handful of top leaders had gone to Nuremberg, where some of them hung, some of them faced prison, and a few had somehow escaped justice.

Zinoviy was generally concerned with the smaller names. Those mid- and senior-ranking officers who had executed the orders resulting in the many war crimes. The ones with literal blood on their hands, rather than merely metaphorical.

Churchill had given his now-famous speech on the *Sinews of Peace* on 5 March 1946, at Westminster College in Fulton, Missouri. Three years ago, now. His proclamation of an Iron Curtain had come to be.

At Berlin, the Americans and their allies had drawn a line in the sand and managed to feed that city for a year with nothing but aircraft and determined anger.

Zinoviy had actually been surprised when it had not devolved into another war, deliberate or otherwise. But Moscow had stepped back from the precipice. Had understood that things could get out of hand and allowed the Western Allies to have their propaganda victory while dragging a few East German politicians back by the chain.

Comrade Stalin would never allow Germany to be reunited. To threaten an invasion of Russia again.

The Israelis were quietly hunting escaped Nazis on some list that was probably rather similar to Zinoviy's. They would welcome the outcomes, but not the assistance. Similarly, the Americans would continue to be utterly implacable to Soviet agents working in their backyard.

So it had been necessary to create the Red Branch instead. Zinoviy's brainchild. Gennadi's work.

Sasha's impossibly good luck. Hopefully, Major Kryvenko

had not exhausted his, because he would need it with what was coming.

Zinoviy reread the newspaper article about the Red Branch. Only the faintest details on the Silver Eagle weapon itself, but Keldysh and his new institute were supposedly working on some sort of similar prototype from the original work of Sänger and Bredt.

Sasha and Gradskaya had saved Washington, D.C. from being bombed. Just as they had saved New York City previously.

The Americans had finally taken notice. Had recruited the Red Branch, though even Gennadi had only the faintest hints how as yet, it being impossible to send a telegram or radio signal that wasn't intercepted.

From hints in other departments, here in Moscow and other places, the Americans and British were reading far more Soviet encryption than they let on, and this secret was too big, too important, to allow it to come out.

He sighed as his cigarette got crushed out, flipping back to the other file.

GRU assassination teams had been activated on somebody's order. Possibly Stalin himself, because the man had a terrible rage when focused. But it didn't really matter.

From deepest cover in America and Britain, someone had ordered the Red Branch destroyed. Publicly. Messily, even.

Zinoviy understood the logic. Kryvenko and the others had all been arrested as part of their cover. Tried and sentenced for treason. Death in Kryvenko's case. Lifetimes in Siberia for the others.

Somehow, all had managed miraculous escapes to the West, where they had supposedly been recruited to join the Red

Branch, which had then gone on to save the world twice. At least as that fool reporter phrased it.

Zinoviy didn't suppose the man was wrong. Understated, if anything, because either of those Werewolf Legion attacks might have been the spark that set off the next global inferno.

And nobody but him and Gennadi knew the truth. And that one would never speak of it. Zinoviy had selected the man for exactly that reason.

What did the Motherland need of him?

Zinoviy shook his head and sighed.

He could not save the Red Branch, without destroying it by telling people who would eventually leak those secrets, either intentionally or merely because they did not know any better.

All that work would vanish in a puff of smoke. Some of the most loyal soldiers, the most capable comrades Gennadi had been able to find, gone.

And there was nothing he could do to prevent it.

CHAPTER 2

Gennadi had dressed a little nicer than normal today. He occasionally missed his uniform as a Colonel of the Soviet Air Forces but understood that he was unlikely to be wearing it again. Possibly ever, depending on how successful today turned out to be.

Thus, a formal blue suit in a darker shade than the Red Branch uniforms and cut in an Italian style. Navy, he seemed to remember it called in the West. White shirt. The crimson tie was his only subtle nod to the land of his birth.

Around him, the factory and small air base he had purchased and caused to be built was silent, as everyone had spent the last two days cleaning and adjusting things, and then had today and tomorrow as something of an extra holiday, with most of the staff home with their families and friends.

Red Branch Command was welcoming important guests, and even the rudest and most patriotic Irish employees were on their best behavior.

Finding people who hated the English in Dublin had been like swinging a dead cat. Especially after the Nazis had gotten a little carried away with their bombing a few times. Filtering those down to loyal comrades who could keep their mouths shut had been a bit harder, but this was not a proper factory. Nor air base. Less than one hundred people worked here at present.

Though today hinted that more was in the offing.

A knock at his door, and Yefim opened it a moment later.

"Spotters in the southwest have identified them, sir," Yefim said, then ducked out.

Gennadi rose. By the door, he found the Swiss-style hat and silver-topped cane that had become part of his everyday costume. The cane was generally unnecessary, but there were days when his war injuries flared up, so he always had it with him. Similarly, his left arm was better these days, but he might never drive a stick-shift car again. Automatics, however, made it easy.

He drew a breath and smiled as he exited his corner office, then down the stairs carefully and out into the courtyard. Again, he could have lived on the ground floor, but Gennadi liked to push himself.

The only way to stay as healthy as he could for as long as possible. Forty-eight was not ancient. It merely felt it some days when the Irish wind was chill and the fog had hungry fingers.

Outside, he heard the buzzing hum as an aircraft came around and lined up with the runway.

Curtiss C-46 *Commando*. A heavier transport aircraft than the more popular Douglas-built C-47 *Skytrain*. Flying from Washington, D.C. with a refueling stop in St. John's, Newfoundland.

US Air Force aircraft. Formerly US Army Air Forces during the war. It had the roundel on the tail.

Gennadi watched it land with a flutter of trepidation in his stomach that he immediately crushed, then began walking towards the car where Yefim was already set to drive. Gennadi let him, getting in back like a Party bigshot, and they crossed to where the Commando had come to rest and turned sideways. Ground crews were already there in a truck, setting chocks and preparing to refuel.

It would be a big day.

CHAPTER 3

Sasha watched the car approach as the pilot shut his engines down. As he unbuckled to stand, Brigadier General Lockwood Carlyle did the same, their blue uniforms different enough that you would not confuse them.

The Red Branch wore a belted tunic with a crossover bib like an extended double-breasted blazer. Medium blue. Matching pants. Calf boot with a walking thread in a polished black leather like his belt.

Sasha had left off the Shanxi Type 17 and holster today, as he was returning to Red Branch Command with an important guest and potential employer that might forever alter the course of what Sasha and the others did in the West.

He made his way aft, leading Carlyle, then went down the steps to the tarmac. Gennadi greeted them there in his jaunty had and smile. Sasha matched it.

"Gennadi, this is General Carlyle, whom I have mentioned," Sasha introduced them. "General, Gennadi Nazarenko, Base Commander, Red Branch Command."

It was odd, but Gennadi had insisted that Sasha was in supreme command, at least in public. Privately, it was more of an equal partnership that left him comfortable, but even then Sasha had to make decisions on the fly, in the field, with little information.

Gut instinct, as he had been warned would be necessary.

The two older men shook hands. Warmly, it seemed.

Around them, the flight crew debarked and would be carried to the mess hall for food and a nap while ground crews worked on any servicing the craft needed. It flew wonderfully. Reasonable range. Excessive capacity, that the General had suggested might be important.

"General, it is good to meet you finally," Gennadi was saying. "I have not heard much of Sasha's latest adventure save what I have read in various newspapers, after he and *Banshee* took off and the rest of the team fled into the brush, before slipping into Brazil."

"I'm just sorry that the Legion got away," Carlyle nodded. "We will find them. I have contacts back home and in London scouring the globe."

"Best not to mention London too loudly, sir," Gennadi offered.

"Oh?"

"We'll talk in the car," Gennadi said. "Come."

Sasha rode up front with Yefim after getting the other two in back.

Yefim drove sedately.

"London?" Carlyle asked.

"We are in Independent Ireland, General," Gennadi offered. "They still remember their own civil war, barely a generation ago, as well as centuries of suffering under the English."

Sasha nodded, listening. It made almost the perfect place to build a factory, where the locals tended to be insular, and enemies of the United Kingdom.

"Was that what caused you to come here?" Carlyle asked.

"It was one reason," Gennadi demurred. "Quiet. Neutral. Desirous of industrial investment, which the Red Branch brought."

"They don't fly jets here," Carlyle noted.

"I believe they will at some point," Sasha offered from the front seat. "The nation is not entirely antagonistic to the UK, as long as London understands that they are peers now, instead of servants. At the same time, without the Nazi menace, there is space for everyone to get along, though possibly at arm's length for a time."

Hopefully, those fools in Westminster understood that. Sasha had read a few reports about how close Churchill had come to violating Ireland's neutrality and forcibly occupying the country, instead of asking politely.

But then, Churchill had always been a bull in a china shop. Still, his example, perhaps, had done more to shape the war and the aftermath than anything, so Sasha would grant him his place on the pedestal. He had held firm, and gotten the Americans more involved than they would have, early enough to make a difference.

Sasha always wondered if the Americans would have let Hitler conquer all of Europe, had the Japanese not rashly attacked. And done so the very day after the Soviet counterattack had stopped the Wehrmacht just short of the gates of Moscow.

Yefim got them to the door and Sasha escorted them into what Gennadi called his boardroom. All wood paneling and comfort. Large table for supposed group meetings, when it had been Gennadi and four pilots at most.

Still, appearances.

It was after lunch, so Sasha joined Carlyle in a highball glass of Irish whiskey on the rocks. An acquired taste, after a lifetime of vodka, but necessary, given their location.

They sat and smiled.

"General, welcome to Ireland," Gennadi said grandly. "Without knowing your arrival time, we are merely prepared. Lunch? A tour of the factory? What would serve your needs best?"

Carlyle turned a wary eye towards Sasha and got a nod. They had danced carefully around certain topics. Hints leavened with misdirections and lies.

As one did when one was a spy. Even in a pretty, blue uniform and a small team of jets.

Carlyle nodded to himself and faced Gennadi.

"We've looked, but there are no clear answers, sir," Carlyle began. "The Red Branch appears to have come into existence fully formed. Or at least, Sasha and Yuri first, with *Banshee* and the one known as Zaslavsky coming later. How did that happen?"

Gennadi nodded soberly.

Sasha held his breath.

CHAPTER 4

Gennadi even smiled. Sasha knew bits, but had been deliberately kept in the dark so that he could not be caught in lies later. As it was, today's story would become the truth of the thing, though it was no more true than any of the other tales.

"I was approached by certain elements," Gennadi began quietly, weaving ambiguity and shadow like threads. "Comrade Stalin is old. The maneuvering to replace him has begun, but that will be years in the completion. Someone was in a position to initiate another purge. Are you familiar with how those things work, General?"

"Only loosely," Carlyle replied.

From the look in his eyes, Carlyle was also lying, but Gennadi presumed that someone had done an adequate job of briefing the man.

Incomplete, likely, but adequate.

"Someone denounces someone else," Gennadi said. "You don't go after your primary target initially, but instead one of his key subordinates. Accuse them of some terrible crime and get the authorities to subject them to arrest and detention. It creates questions about the competence of the superior.

Someone wanted one of my bosses removed. Presumably to promote one of their people instead."

He paused there and waited for a nod. Obvious, on the face of it, if one had spent any time in any competent bureaucracy. Only in the Soviet Union it was done with knives. Only sometimes were they metaphorical ones.

Sometimes.

"In 1946, during the demobilization, I was targeted," Gennadi continued. "Chased out, if you will, even as I had finally recovered from my injuries suffered during the last weeks of the war and was ready to return to duty fully."

"Plane crash?" Carlyle asked.

"After a tremendous duel lasting almost half an hour," Gennadi smiled. "With the man who would later go on to become the head of the Werewolf Legion, Alois Voss. That, however, was pure luck. Or the gods with some dark sense of humor, as I had believed him dead, based on reports in the aftermath. My Lavochkin La-7 managed to limp as far as friendly lines, where I was pulled from the burning wreckage by a Guards Tank unit."

"Got it," Carlyle nodded.

He did not have the look of a man who had ever been shot down, but Gennadi didn't know his background.

"When I was cast out, I managed to escape, with the help of certain benefactors," Gennadi lied smoothly. And it wasn't even entirely a lie. "They offered funds that I am given to understand came from Nazi gold that got lost somewhere along the way, in the insanity that accompanied the last days of the war. Because I already knew aircraft, they suggested a thing. I shaped it into the Red Branch, because I knew that I had been merely the first victim, and that others would come later. Thus, I was able to rescue Sasha and Yuri when the commissars took aim at them. Vanya, Lyuba, and Pavel later. The enlisted men and woman were easier, because few of them had been accused of anything grand or grotesque."

"Do you know who backed you?" Carlyle asked.

Gennadi noted the way that both Sasha and the American leaned in.

Gennadi shrugged like an actor.

"There were hints at the time of British Intelligence," he lied, casting the net so wide that it would capture every fish in the pond if someone went looking. "I have received a few messages since, suggesting possibly White Russians in exile. And mayhap Americans, but that might be a lie intended to confuse me. It was more important to rescue the pilots I could. Folks I knew. The plans for building the Vampire were made available, and we were able to even build in improvements, partly because the British are functionally broke today and willing to accept bribes. Glorious plans in a variety of files. No money to actually construct most of them, though they still try. They must stick with basic designs, instead of funding various prototypes. Because we currently only have four working aircraft and two spares, I have more options available."

He left it at that, watching the man's eyes.

They didn't need to know how utterly riddled British Intelligence and the government itself were with deep cover Soviet agents, including a few, per Zinoviy, that were supposed to be watching for infiltrators themselves.

Quis custodiet ipsos custodes?

Who watches the watchers? All the more reason Zinoviy kept him beyond arm's length. Otherwise, someone might stumble over the truth in those games in the shadows.

Carlyle leaned back, pensive. Gennadi waited.

The entire mission—everything he had spent several years preparing—might fall apart right here.

Or it might gain the protection and assistance of the Americans.

Those gods, with their black humor indeed.

"And recruiting more pilots?" Carlyle asked warily.

Gennadi shrugged.

"At the moment, I suspect that the authorities in Moscow are churning hard to discover how Sasha and the others fled from justice," he offered. "That pipeline might dry up. However, because we are public, and have had certain publicity as a result of Mr. Walker at the newspaper, I have been quietly contacted by certain international individuals. Most have been glory seekers, but I have ruthlessly filtered that stack of inquiries down to meet my conditions, before showing it to Sasha. He will make the final decisions."

As he should. Any of those people would be in the air with him, flying combat missions. He would have to trust them with his life. With all their lives.

And keep a whole second set of books at the same time.

"I might have a few names for you to review," Carlyle replied. "And call me Lockwood, when we're in less formal circumstances."

Gennadi managed to keep his jaw from falling open, but only barely. If that was the case, the Americans might be serious about hiring the Red Branch. Funding them to something far grander than Gennadi had been able to do, Nazi gold or not.

The Nazis had looted every nation they had conquered. Stolen all the gold from their banks. And their populations.

Then there was what they did to the Jews.

Gennadi was not a religious man. Like Sasha, he liked to

think of himself as the embodiment of the *New Soviet Man*, leading the world into a bright future beyond aristocracy and religion, like that one French philosopher, Diderot, had suggested.

What the Nazis had done to the Jews was enough for Gennadi to kill all of them he could find, regardless of who might be protecting them.

The Red Branch in America opened up a number of options for justice, however delayed.

"I welcome your submissions, General," Gennadi replied. "As I said, we have three aircraft without pilots at present, though only two need radar operators, as Nikon has been exceptional. My list has a handful to consider, plus yours."

"How long is the Nightviper still at the leading edge?" Carlyle asked.

Gennadi nodded and allowed himself a bit of a sigh.

"It is as good as it can get, in its current form," he replied. "Sasha has previously test piloted the MiG-15, and has, so I have been given to understand, flown your new Sabrejet a few times to compare them, even as Vanya and Lyuba assist in that today."

"Sasha thinks those two are comparable, almost across the board," Carlyle offered.

"Then he is probably correct," Gennadi said. "I have seen plans for a new version called the Venom that replaces the Vampire. And a navalized version, with swept wings, dual engines, and other improvements. de Havilland is working slowly on it for the Royal Navy but might be years from actually being able to fly the design."

"Because the Brits are broke," Carlyle nodded.

"Indeed," Gennadi agreed. "They have those wonderfully vast libraries of designs. And some of the best people in the world to come up with the future. Their eyes are larger than their stomachs, as the old saying goes."

Carlyle started to say something, but a sound caught Gennadi's attention. Took him back to the war, stirring up sudden and uncomfortable memories.

A hand came up, demanding silence.

"Everyone, under the table!" he snapped, pushing his chair back and falling. "NOW!"

Sasha moved quickly. Carlyle was a moment longer, then managed to get to cover.

Then the world exploded.

CHAPTER 5

GRU General Taras Chaykovsky studied the man across the desk from him. Colonel Kazimir Matveev, *Spetsnatz GRU,* a new special operations unit formed this year under orders from the very top.

Matveev was a hard man. A veteran of the Great Patriotic War who had handled many missions behind Nazi lines as the Germans were slowly driven back, kilometer over kilometer. Body over body.

Spetsnatz GRU was a new thing, intended to carry out reconnaissance and sabotage against enemy targets in the form of special long-range patrols and direct-action attacks.

In wartime, Spetsnatz troops would conduct infiltration and insertion behind enemy lines, both in uniform or civilian clothing, usually well before hostilities were scheduled to begin and, once they were in place, to commit acts of sabotage such as the destruction of vital communications and logistics centers, as well as the assassination of key government leaders and military officers.

Hobbling the enemy at that critical moment.

"You understand your target?" Taras asked bluntly.

"The Red Branch," Matveev nodded. "Their base in Ireland is not guarded like it should be, according to my briefing materials. Their teams in America will be more difficult to reach, but I have a second team in place that is ready to be activated if the first one fails, though I am not entirely certain why we do not launch simultaneous assaults, Comrade General."

"Kryvenko and Nazarenko are the key elements," Taras replied. "The Kremlin wishes them eliminated. Gradskaya flew the Silver Eagle, and thus has information and experience critical to the Motherland and many scientists here in Moscow and other places wish to learn it. Zhidkov was a commissar. Both of those will need to be returned to Russia for interrogation and possible punishment. Our planners do not believe that you can exfiltrate them from Muroc Air Force Base in California without killing them, so you will watch, and take them when they leave those confines. If you are successful in Ireland, our expectation is that the rest of the Red Branch will be cast out by the Americans as a security risk. Kryvenko is the one that interests them."

Matveev nodded.

"What are your plans, Colonel?" Taras asked.

"The British will sell surplus military equipment to anyone with cash, almost no questions asked," the man smiled. "This will allow us to initiate all manner of confusion and accusations later, when the Irish government is led to believe that the British have returned to their old ways. Thus, chaos is injected in addition to everything else."

"Just beware that the Americans are also involved and interested," Taras noted. "One of theirs is accompanying Kryvenko to Ireland."

"All the more reason for *Perfidious Albion* to take the

blame," Matveev smiled. "It was Churchill that demanded the West push back, where Atlee has sought to remain friendly with the Soviet Union. Perhaps this drives a wedge in that relationship as well."

"As long as you understand, Colonel," Taras nodded.

"The flight crew will vanish afterwards," Matveev replied. "I have a ship in the North Atlantic off Northern Ireland ready to pick them up when they ditch, and the aircraft itself will vanish entirely under the waves. After bombing Dublin, they will turn North, thus further implicating the British."

Taras nodded. His people were already breaking covers well established to do this, but the orders had been specific, and bombing the base had been the best way to achieve them, since having combat aircraft loitering nearby would have drawn suspicion.

"As long as it works," he reminded Matveev. "This is only stage one."

There were other teams in America that were being activated as well.

So much effort, but Kryvenko was an enemy of the state.

He must be punished for it.

CHAPTER 6

Makar Kovalyov had flown many American and British aircraft during the Great Patriotic War. Afterwards, he had been inserted into Britain under cover to become a spy.

By day, he made a living flying cargo between various locations faster than it could be sent by boat. Thus, he had access to all the right skills and equipment, though he had never expected something like this.

Still, orders were orders. And a truck had arrived with the weapons he needed, a set of eight RP-3 rockets, plus the rails to mount them on the old de Havilland Mosquito he kept in a secure hangar, supposedly demilitarized, but not really. It still had the four 20mm Hispano cannons that had been the late-war version for hunting Nazi aircraft.

And the rockets were the Number Two, Mark I. Flat-angle weapons designed to destroy tanks from low altitude. They worked equally well against buildings.

They were flying out over the Irish Sea, he and Varfolomei Vasiliev in the bomber/navigator station. Circling and out of sight, ready to pounce.

"Dagger, this is Merchant," the call came over the radio.

"Package located and confirmed. Location Three. Repeat, Three."

"Merchant, this is Dagger," Makar replied. "Confirming location three, over."

"See you shortly," Merchant said, then the radio went silent.

Location Three. The office building attached to the factory where they built and serviced the aircraft. Brick and concrete, it would be an excellent target for his missiles, then he could perhaps swing back around and destroy the aircraft on the ground. Nobody knew what the traitor would be flying in today, so they had not attempted to intercept.

His de Havilland Mosquito had been one of the fastest aircraft in the world a decade ago, but jets put that to shame. Better to catch them asleep and bomb them.

"Come to two-nine-zero and climb," Varfolomei said. "That will put us on the vector we want for any radar systems. Later we will shift to roughly two-one-five for the attack."

"Coming around," Makar said.

The Mosquito was a lovely craft. Fast, agile, and deadly today with rockets and guns. He was looking forward to killing a traitor.

CHAPTER 7

Makar was on the final flight vector. In the distance, he could see the runway at Red Branch Command as well as a large transport parked on an apron.

"Arming rockets," Varfolomei said.

"Guns ready for engagement," Makar replied.

"Prepare to dive," Varfolomei ordered. "I am not detecting air defense radar, and Merchant did not identify any anti-aircraft cannons."

"Slow and steady," Makar said, almost laughing.

Fish in a barrel. It took him back to the end of the war, when the Nazi air force had been all but annihilated, and Soviet attack aircraft flew almost at will.

Civilians below, and none of those damnable Nightviper aircraft that were supposedly as good as anything in the air.

Even he could not stand up to a combat jet. Not in a Mosquito, as much as he loved the old bird and would be sad to see it destroyed after this.

Some sacrifices were necessary.

Because there were no defenders on this first pass, he came in slow and smooth, dipping his nose like he was about to land on the runway, before adjusting to his right and lining up on the building.

"A little more right and down," Varfolomei said. "There. Hold that and stand by to launch."

Makar nodded, concentrating on flying.

Gorgeous day. Breeze out of the west and no clouds. Warm skies below.

He could see airmen working on the transport all stop and look up at him. Confused. Surprised. Something.

"Fire your first volley," Varfolomei said.

Makar reached out and sent four rockets into the building from optimal range. Automatically, he pulled the accelerator and sped up, rolling away to his right to make a second pass with the other four.

Old wartime habits that had kept him alive.

From the northwest this time. Bodies were running every which way below as he came in low. Nobody had weapons to fire back, so the second set of rockets went off smoothly.

This time, roll to the left and circle.

A third pass, and he hammered that transport on the ground for no other reason than it was there. And the ground crews had all wisely fled by now, so the ones outside should be safe. They were Irish. Working for the traitor, but otherwise innocent enough.

Well, they were Irish, and he'd spent enough time around the English to have picked up some of their disdain for their neighbors. Folks inside the office building might be in trouble. It looked to have partially collapsed. Burning in a few place, but that might be the explosives more than anything.

"Any other targets?" Makar asked.

"Negative," Varfolomei replied. "Come to zero-one-five and accelerate as you stay low. That puts us roughly on a path over Belfast for our escape. I don't know if British air defenses will be scrambled, but we'll fly below radar."

"They don't like the Irish either," Makar reminded him. "Someone over there might give us a medal."

"We have to get home first."

Makar nodded and aimed to the north, with one quick glance back at the rubble and smoke he was leaving behind.

All in a day's work.

CHAPTER 8

Sasha greatly appreciated the sturdy conference table when part of a wall collapsed and it held.

"What was that?" he asked Gennadi, checking that General Carlyle—Lockwood—was safe nearby.

"Rockets," Gennadi replied. "Fired from an aircraft at low altitude. Better than the old dive bombers everyone used before the war."

Sasha cursed. He had thought—no, assumed—that Red Branch Command in Neutral Ireland would be safe, but he'd been thinking in terms of national actors. Not terrorists.

Two salvos of those damnable rockets. Then someone killing Lockwood's Commando with cannon fire.

Now silence.

They crawled from under the wreckage of the room, sky visible on his right where an entire wall had collapsed.

Smoke. Presumably fire.

Sasha pulled Gennadi to his shaky feet. Lockwood joined them as Sasha walked to the hole in the wall. Irish crew were running towards him with fire extinguishers and rescue gear, but Sasha stepped over a knee-high wall of brick as they arrived.

He noted a dot in the northern sky, receding quickly.

Sasha turned to Gennadi.

"Is Red-5 prepped to fly?" he asked.

"It is," Gennadi replied.

"Armed?"

"Yes, because having a possible demonstration today was on my list."

"I'm going after him," Sasha said simply. "And killing him. Whoever he is."

Gennadi started to reply, then stopped himself and turned to one of the men nearby.

"Get the commander airborne immediately," Gennadi ordered.

The man blinked for an instant, then nodded.

"This way, sir," he said.

Sasha started to jog in the man's wake. Three steps passed and he noted that Lockwood was keeping pace.

"I'm going with you," Lt. General Carlyle announced. "You'll need someone operating your radar systems."

He had a point. Sasha could have done it well enough, but it still required three hands to manage. And Lockwood was current on a lot of systems, in his shadowy role as an aviation consultant for the US Government and various agencies beyond merely the Air Force.

Sasha kept up his jog.

Red-5 was in a hangar that had been ignored when the Commando got shattered. And the main building.

Sasha assumed an assassination attempt, probably aimed at him, since nobody knew who Lockwood was. At least nobody was supposed to.

Perhaps they wanted to wipe out the entire Red Branch Command at once? He did not spend much time in Dublin, but that was the need to be in the field. South America initially. California today.

Red-5 was fueled and ready. Sasha presumed that someone had done a thorough pre-flight and simply climbed in.

"Start us up," he yelled over the noise of fire sirens in the distance, the locals no doubt responding to the smoke as he got his helmet on and adjusted.

Lockwood was in the seat where Ilya would normally be. Or Nikon, more recently.

The engines started with a bang and his crew withdrew to safety. Sasha brought them up enough to guide the small jet out into the sunlight, already at one end of the runway.

The Vampire upon which his Nightviper was based was a tiny aircraft. Especially as he'd been test flying F-86 Sabrejets for Lockwood most recently. The Sabre was huge. A whale, while this was a barracuda.

Just as deadly.

Sasha eyeballed the immediate vicinity. Nobody on the runway or verge. No aircraft preparing to land.

Open skies.

He turned onto the strip and opened the throttle, immediately accelerating and then pulling back and leaping into the sky.

"He went north," Sasha said to his partner. "Find him."

"Working on it now," Lockwood replied. "Do we need to notify anyone?"

"I don't want them knowing I'm coming," Sasha said grimly.

CHAPTER 9

Sasha saw the dot in the distance. He'd initially gone high, using the Nightviper's upgraded power to get to elevation, but there had been no aircraft headed away from the base.

Lockwood had fiddled as they dropped lower, though, and found a target. Hiding. Not tree-top, but such that ground radars would be hard-pressed to see him for more than a moment as he raced by.

But he also couldn't run fast enough to escape the Nightviper.

It took Sasha back to the war to see a de Havilland Mosquito flying. Painted in British colors. Moving at high speed for being barely five hundred meters off the deck.

Running.

A decade ago, it had been one of the fastest production aircraft in the world. Useful, during the war. And infinitely flexible, to the point that it had been used as a low- to medium-altitude daytime tactical bomber, high-altitude night bomber, pathfinder, day or night fighter, fighter-bomber, intruder, maritime strike, and photo-reconnaissance aircraft. Almost everything.

Truly, wondrous.

Sadly out of date today.

"That's him," Lockwood said confidently. "Matches every-thing, assuming running away from attacking your base."

Sasha nodded and nosed over. The Nightviper could not break the sound barrier. No straight-winged aircraft could, as far as he knew. It took swept wings. Or rockets like the American X-1 that Yeager had used.

He had to dial back the power as he swooped in behind the Mosquito. That one was cruising at what was probably his top speed, but it still felt like walking to Sasha.

"What's the plan?" Lockwood asked.

"I cannot open fire on a random aircraft," Sasha replied after a moment. "Let us see how he reacts to company."

They would be over Northern Ireland soon at this rate, but they were over water now. Flying a reciprocal to Belfast, though he had no idea if they were landing there or merely overflying.

He did slip below the Mosquito, using his test piloting skills to sneak up behind where he could see the launch rails on the wings.

Again, not entirely a giveaway.

Not if he was about to open fire. It might be an innocent pilot out for a day flight, with an old Mosquito. Sasha hadn't see the actual attacker up close, and none of the ground crew had mentioned anything, so intent on either fighting the fire or getting him airborne to get revenge.

He hadn't even stayed to determine the number of causalities, but there was nothing he could do for them that Gennadi couldn't do better.

Except avenge them.

"Rails for rocket launchers?" Lockwood asked.

"It appears so," Sasha replied. "Time to say hello."

"You aren't just opening up?"

Sasha had the impression that he'd surprised the general, but Red Branch was generally not a place to shoot first and ask questions later.

Except in certain circumstances. Nazi bedrooms and the like.

Sasha pulled the throttle and flared off to his left, slipping up to a level with the Mosquito and coming even as he matched their speed.

Two-person cockpit, side by side, just like the Nightviper. Sasha saw it, the instant the bomber/navigator spotted him. The head came around. A hand pointed across the pilot's face.

The Mosquito pilot pitched over into a dive.

Sasha nodded.

Not a lot of doubt at this point. Man should have cut his speed to almost nothing to stall. Sasha was certain that a Nightviper had to fly faster or fall out of the sky.

Of course, that would only buy them a few moments and leave them vulnerable.

He nosed over and began to chase.

CHAPTER 10

Sasha trailed the Mosquito out of the sky, but there wasn't much space to maneuver at this low altitude, so he stayed back, letting a gap develop between them.

Sure enough, the pilot leveled off quickly and rolled onto his left wing.

"He's going for land," Lockwood called.

Sasha nodded and followed. Idly, he wondered if anybody had a parachute today. He hadn't taken the time. The crew might not have packed any sort of emergency gear on Red-5, but the people who bombed his base had obviously prepared ahead of time, so they might.

Then they were dogfighting. The Mosquito wasn't as nimble as some of the craft he'd flown. Heavy-duty, for other chores.

The Vampire that was the basis for the Nightviper had been amazingly nimble. The Red Branch had upgraded a number of things to make it even better.

The Sabrejet and the MiG-15 could both run faster. The Sabre could break the sound barrier in a dive.

Sasha could maneuver with either of them at any altitude.

He came up and off to one side of the Mosquito, firing a hard burst of 23mm shells across and ahead the Mosquito's nose. Tracers in there, so a bright line cut the afternoon sky but missed impacting.

Warning shot.

An innocent man would lower his gear as a surrender. Or do something to show that he wasn't a threat.

The Mosquito pilot pulled back on his stick and took the aircraft into a sharp wingover, snapping up and then turning flat like a car, before diving and leveling off again, this time pointed back out to sea low enough that crashing was a risk.

Sasha stayed with him. The Nightviper was a better aircraft. He didn't think the pilot over there was all that sharp, either. War veteran pilot, likely, but four years out of practice in combat flying, while Sasha had stayed with it since the Nazis had been destroyed.

And a test pilot.

In a fresh Nightviper.

"Now what?" Lockwood asked.

Sasha nodded. He was used to Ilya's calm quiet in the other seat.

"Now, I have given him several chances to not be the man who bombed Red Branch Command," Sasha replied evenly as the Mosquito continued to yaw, skip, and pitch, mostly keeping on a random path that made it hard to keep guns centered on him.

There wasn't much a Mosquito could do in this situation, away from help that might chase Sasha off.

"Don't think you have to worry about that," Lockwood offered blandly. "And whatever you do, remember that you have a US Air Force General in the cockpit with you. The Brits might bitch, but a lot less, because I can make a few calls later."

Sasha nodded and concentrated on his foe.

It was weird, possibly having the military might of the United States behind him. The entire concept of the Red Branch was to work outside the auspices of the Soviet Union, because the Iron Curtain made certain things impossible.

What were his limits now?

"Engaging," Sasha said unnecessarily.

The Mosquito pilot was good enough to have survived the war. But he was not that good. The aircraft had been exceptional.

Yesterday.

Today, the Nightviper slithered back onto his foe's tail and held. Sasha let the man's manic maneuvering show tendencies and habits, even as they both circled, rolled, and cut back and forth.

Sasha waited for the pilot to overcommit and try to recover, sliding Red-5's nose ahead and firing.

The Mosquito was mostly made of wood. Strong and cheap. Brittle when intersecting cannon fire. Most of the metal was in the engines.

Sasha let the Mosquito fly through a long burst, high and left. Smoke immediately started out of the port engine, a black, oily trail as that propeller failed and slowed down.

Rather than risk whatever guns the Mosquito had, Sasha stalled, nose up and air brakes deployed. Just as well, as his foe slowed as well, then nosed over in a controlled dive.

Space developed again.

"You letting him get away?" Lockwood asked.

"No."

Sasha took his time. They were miles off shore where the water ran deep, supposedly a river valley from ancient times when all of this had been dry land, according to some scientists.

Hard to recover wreckage. Not that he cared.

The Mosquito leveled off, but with one engine dead and acting as an air anchor, he was doomed. Sasha gave them a five count, and was about to finish the craft off when the cockpit opened and two men jumped clear.

"I have two parachutes in the air," Lockwood announced.

Good enough.

Sasha shattered the Mosquito with another long burst, lest it stray back over land and hurt someone in crashing.

"Red Branch Command, this is Carlyle," Sasha heard him call on the radio.

It took a couple of tries, but Gennadi was on the radio.

"This is Red Branch Command."

Lockwood transmitted a set of coordinates that Sasha assumed were correct as he put the craft into a wide circle. He'd been busy flying.

"Contact Irish Coast Guard and Royal Navy and tell them to expect two crashed pilots in the water at this location," Lockwood continued.

"Roger that, Carlyle. Stand by."

The General flipped a switch and they were local again.

"Do we stay?"

Sasha considered it, but all he could do would be to circle until fuel concerns forced him back to base.

Which would be long before any rescue ships could arrive.

"No," Sasha decided. "We'll head home and sort out that mess next. I might call on you when the Irish authorities arrive demanding answers."

"I'll blame English terrorists, if I have to," Lockwood replied.

Sasha glanced over sharply, but the man was smiling.

"I'd prefer if all this got smothered under some sort of Official Secrets Act legalities," Sasha said.

Lockwood sobered.

"Yeah, that might be the best idea," he said. "I'll send a message to the embassy in Dublin and ask for them to contact the Pentagon. Going to need transportation when this is all done."

Sasha nodded and lined up with the base in his mind. Being able to locate a spot on the invisible horizon and fly directly towards it had been one of the reasons he had been assigned to ferry aircraft out of the desert, after the Nazis had been driven from Africa. Faster than crossing Siberia from Montana by far.

"Sasha, your base is not secure if they want to try this again," Lockwood offered quietly. "Have you considered moving everything to the US?"

Sasha was glad that he had to concentrate on flying, so he didn't turn to the man with his jaw hinged open like a snake.

Americans working on his craft? Or worse, building him something new, since the previous conversation had been about how the Nightviper was going to be surpassed by other craft soon.

Not immediately, because the new F-94s being built by the US Air Force were only *almost as good* as his Nightviper, being an adaptation of the Lockheed T-33 Shooting Star that was itself an adaptation of the older P-80 Shooting Star that was already being phased out in favor of newer aircraft.

Every year, it seemed, there was another revolution in jets that made last year's craft yesterday's news.

And the Nightviper would be there soon.

"What does that cost me, General?" Sasha asked. "I can see

the benefits, but Ireland is Neutral and so not anybody's direct enemy."

"Either the Werewolf Legion has just popped back up on radar, or your old comrades in Moscow have decided that you're too popular, Sasha," Lockwood answered. "Either way, we can protect you a lot better there. And if my friends in the civilian world are serious about funding your operations out of their black budgets, it gives you flexibility. I doubt that anyone would complain about you moving under these circumstances."

"I feel like I should contact Addison Walker and give him another exclusive," Sasha laughed. "Let him tell the story of this attack, once we know what happened and how to hide certain things."

"That is not the worst idea I have heard, Sasha," Lockwood replied. "You probably need more people on your side, and this is a good way to do it. Hell, have you considered going on a speaking tour? You and Lyuba, talking about the Red Branch and some of your adventures. Good way to move you around, too, if we needed to have you available for a mission when we find who did this."

"Or they know where to come after us, once you put up posters," Sasha countered.

"Bring your whole team," Lockwood got serious. "Everyone. And we'll see about what other experts I need to locate to fill in spots, because Gennadi gave you an amazingly diverse and competent ground unit, in addition to expert pilots. Let's extend that."

Sasha was aghast that it might be that easy. That they might be installed at the very center of the American intelligence apparatus when he wanted to hunt his old foes.

At the same time, he wasn't GRU. And Gennadi had said

that they were to operate entirely in isolation, save for when messages could be gotten to them. Or when General Shuysky had traveled to Dublin with verbal orders.

There was no way that would happen in California.

At least he didn't think so. Who knew what the GRU could do if they set their minds to it?

"We will talk to Gennadi," Sasha temporized. "About half of the base staff might be necessary, wherever we go."

"There are all sorts of options available," Lockwood said. "Up to possibly naturalizing your folks if necessary."

Sasha set the autopilot before his hands started shaking too much.

A US citizen?

Alice had once fallen down a rabbit hole. He understood her so much better today.

First step, get back to base and see how bad the damage had been.

CHAPTER 11

Gennadi was out on the grass, leaning on his cane because it would take the weight on his shoulders.

Across the way, an Irish fire unit was poking and prodding at things, but the rockets had not been incendiary, so not a lot had caught fire and his own people had killed all their fire extinguishers making sure.

People had been hurt, but nobody seriously, which both astounded and pleased him. The building was probably a loss. Fortunately, he kept the important papers in an underground vault that had been designed and built by folks paranoid about the recent war. And he could still get down there, once everything was secure and excavated.

It helped that he had taken a much larger office building than he needed, with space for all the pilots and a larger staff that he had not recruited yet.

The building could be destroyed and not impact his operations all that much.

In the distance, he heard that particular roaring whine that marked a Nightviper in flight. Gennadi turned and picked them out, just starting to circle before landing, but the runway was clear.

The Commando was probably a total loss as well, because someone had strafed it professionally and repair parts would have to be brought in, either by truck or another cargo aircraft. And possibly mechanics that knew the craft, though his people had been exceptional at adapting to new equipment.

Red-5 landed smoothly and taxied back into the hangar before shutting things down. The ground crews quickly went to work.

Yefim appeared from somewhere, possibly supervising things from the smudges of smoke and dirt on his face and pants.

"Walk with me," Gennadi said before Yefim even opened his mouth to suggest they ride.

It wasn't far, and his aches and pains would be well served with the exercise. Yefim shrugged and they walked.

Sasha and the American general met them at the bay door.

"Everything well?" Gennadi asked, mostly *pro forma* because various naval forces were in motion to locate the other flight crew.

And arrest them.

"It flies well," Carlyle opined. "In the hands of an expert. The radar system is probably the oldest portion, but it worked for my needs."

Gennadi had been concerned about the man, but his body language spoke of a new friendliness that hadn't even been there before they left.

"Someone will be looking for the others," Gennadi said.

They fell in and headed to the intact main barracks. Gennadi had never bothered getting any sort of flat off the base, though many of his employees lived in local villages, some with families. And today, most of them had been safely at home, instead of where they might have gotten hurt. More importantly for him. it had a commissary that would do, with dinner not that far off.

"What happens now?" Gennaci asked, uncertain what Sasha and Carlyle had talked about today.

Both before arriving here and after they'd gone hunting.

Sasha nodded to Carlyle.

"He suggests that Ireland might not be safe for us," Sasha began. "That perhaps we will need to move elsewhere, because I cannot imagine that the locals would appreciate us installing air defense cannons. Nor the sudden need."

"I would second that idea," Gennadi nodded. "They were willing to accept us for the money we brought, the technological skills we taught, and the fact that we were otherwise quiet about things. The latter is probably gone."

He paused and glanced across to the man walking on Sasha's other wing.

"Where would we go?"

"Most of the team is currently at Muroc, outside Los Angeles," Carlyle replied. "I need to talk to my people on a variety of topics, but that's a location that might serve our various needs."

Gennadi glanced at Sasha and caught a nod, so they had spoken on the topic previously.

Gennadi kept a chuckle inside.

Unlike the others, he had been GRU before all this. Technically, he still was, operating deep-cover and long-term, entirely outside the control of any superiors because they had made enough money in South America to operate for a while yet. Plus the Americans had deposited funds in various banks for Sasha's services.

He wasn't about to break away from Mother Russia, but California offered all manner of new opportunities to hunt Nazi war criminals.

First, though, whoever had ordered this raid needed to be killed like a mad dog, their body left in the ditch afterwards for the buzzards to eat.

"How is the base?" Sasha asked as they got close.

Gennadi looked around, but Yefim had vanished from sight.

The man was good at that sort of thing. It made him an excellent assistant and personal secretary.

"The factory and barracks are fine," Gennadi replied. "They ignored the hangars to kill the Commando. My office might be destroyed, but there was little stored there anyway. I will need to get into the basement to confirm a few things."

"Basement?" Carlyle asked.

"All the important papers and such are in a bomb-proof vault," Gennadi replied. He paused and considered, then took a leap of faith, based on how Carlyle and Sasha seemed to have bonded.

Aerial combat would do that. He could testify.

"The plans for the Nightviper and the Camel," Gennadi replied. "Plus other aircraft and various systems that people have occasionally slipped in via post or messenger. The Nightviper is a British design evolved from the Vampire, with improved engines over the Ghost 103. Similarly, the armaments have been upgraded to Soviet NR-23 cannon that my exiles knew better. As we were discussing before all this occurred, the British have fantastic designers, especially certain folks at Vickers and Miles, over and above what de Havilland has accomplished. What they lack is money to turn those dreams into aircraft."

"What could you do with money?" Carlyle asked abruptly.

"Replace the Nightviper," Gennadi replied carefully, unwilling yet to dream. "We have a variety of thoughts on the topic, but no certainty as to what might be needed. And while the Nightviper is excellent, others have finally begun to catch up, so we need to leap well ahead again."

Was this fool about to offer a black budget over and above the one Gennadi already had?

The smile was in his eyes, but nowhere else.

"I know a guy in California," Carlyle said quietly. "Quite literally a genius at that sort of thing. And the civilians have funds. That might be doubly helpful, as we would like to generally keep our military involvement with the Red Branch to a minimum in public. You folks are mercenaries, obviously, so might need to be hired by folks that wouldn't ask the US Government for assistance. Or like to be seen accepting it."

"Then let us go break bread and drink whiskey, while we tell each other stories and lies, General," Gennadi smiled.

Carlyle matched it. Sasha did as well.

This might be the future of the Red Branch unfolding.

CHAPTER 12

Sasha was still learning to enjoy whiskey. And develop the subtle palate for all the various ways that it might be made, when vodka was far less interesting.

They had eaten. Toasted one another. Told those various stories and lies.

Lockwood had put in a call to Dublin, then they had all sat around and talked of the war. Gennadi had the most interesting stories, but he had been one of those few pilots stationed far enough back from the sudden German invasion at Barbarossa to not have his aircraft destroyed on the first day.

Lockwood had been with the American 8th Air Force, flying the B-17 and then the B-29 Superfortress over Europe.

Sasha had been a taxi pilot. It had been necessary. Only at the end had he and Yuri been called to the front lines, when the Red Army finally had enough aircraft and wanted to annihilate the Luftwaffe.

Still, they had all survived. And stayed with it after most of the armies had been demobilized.

Yefim Zaitsev opened the door to their room.

"General Carlyle, the folks from your embassy are here," he said, then ducked out.

Lockwood rose. Sasha did as well.

"I won't be long," Lockwood told them, waving Sasha to sit again. "Quick tour of the damage to building and aircraft, then a series of messages they'll need to cable to DC. They'll see about getting my flight crew transported home as well."

Sasha nodded and sat as Lockwood pulled the door closed.

"How did your afternoon go?" Gennadi asked.

"He suggested naturalization as a possibility," Sasha said. "And possibly expanded that to the local mechanics that you might need to transport with the factory."

Gennadi's face darkened.

"Can we still hunt war criminals?" the Colonel asked.

"I am not certain," Sasha replied. "Lockwood is fanatic about locating and destroying the Werewolf Legion, but this attack feels like someone else, if only because there would have been a wolfpack, either in the air or on the ground. We got extremely lucky that whoever did this didn't succeed. Or follow up."

"Indeed," Gennadi nodded. "I lean towards taking him up on the offer, but that for my own reasons, which might begin to diverge from yours."

Sasha understood. Gennadi was a spy.

They all were, really, but the rest were a field team intended to hunt renegade Nazi war criminals. Gennadi might want to tell Moscow about things in detail Lockwood was not prepared to understand.

"How far does our cover go?" Sasha asked.

"As far as it needs," Gennadi replied. "I have spoken with my superiors about how your public personas might cause trouble with other things. If that is the case, they are prepared to try other avenues. More specifically, to step back and let us operate, knowing that you and I are unlikely to be seduced by all the West has to offer. At least until we complete our task."

Sasha paused and considered the pilot he'd fought. Competent. Skilled, but out of practice at combat flying. Perhaps by four years?

"If we are unknown, was this someone in Moscow who believes that we are all traitors?" Sasha asked.

Gennadi's eyes grew hard.

"It might be," he agreed. "And nobody who knew the truth could say anything without possibly blowing our cover and ruining everything."

"So we might be hunted by other Soviet agents?" Sasha pressed.

They had spoken of the Mosquito pilot. His tactics. His style.

"That might be a sleeper agent that was activated for this mission," Gennadi replied. "Certainly, whoever it was will be in trouble if he is caught. And a Mosquito taking off will be something someone saw, once the British or Irish get serious about looking."

"Or the Americans," Sasha added.

"So we will assume that they will be caught and subjected to whatever laws apply," Gennadi said. "Are you opposed to basing out of America?"

"I am not," Sasha said. "The work of the Red Branch might change. And it might not. Latin America seems to be a hotbed of chaos, even as East Asia grows more unstable. We might be called upon to fight communist freedom fighters."

"And you will, Sasha," Gennadi ordered. "Whatever the contract calls for. However it is necessary."

Sasha nodded.

It was not the life he could have imagined for himself. At the same time, he had already stopped two major attacks on the United States in the last year, so the job was necessary.

He would do it.

CHAPTER 13

Lockwood Carlyle looked around, but he and Mr. Ingles from the embassy were well away from everyone else. His flight crew were bunking with the Red Branch mechanics for now, because nobody was certain what happened next.

Plane was toast. Hadn't burned, but someone had done a doozy of a job with what looked like 20mm cannons. Maybe repairable, but C-46s were practically a dime a dozen these days, because everybody preferred the smaller and lighter DC-3 variant that had been so ubiquitous.

And the Commando was expensive to fly. Still carried a LOT more cargo though.

"From there, I intend to talk to them about packing most of this up and moving it to California," Lockwood concluded, gesturing at all the various bits around them.

"I shall update the Ambassador," Ingles replied blandly. "He is, however, a political appointee, rather than a career civil servant."

"There is a reason I used the codes to activate you instead," Lockwood said. "This is something that needs to be buried pretty deep. I'm not sure where the line is, but Sasha and his people straddle between military and civilian, and my superiors are interested in how we might use the Red Branch as another weapon nobody knows about. Can't do that if every Tom, Dick, and Harry who comes along might bomb the joint. Or worse, do to Sasha what he did to those Nazis in Paraguay, slipping over the wire to shoot the place up."

"The Irish would be generally opposed to hosting any sort of military base," Ingles acknowledged. "Private or not. American or not. Certainly, the British would not be remotely welcome. They have their portion across the border."

"We don't want to go there," Lockwood said. "If Red Branch Command is moving, it need to be someplace safe."

"So I will convey," Ingles nodded. "How quickly do you need to get back to Washington?"

"Ask them to send a plane big enough to get me and Sasha back," Lockwood replied. "Maybe Nazarenko, too, but that's a little more iffy, if only because he'd need to supervise packing things up here."

"And Irish citizens getting work visas?"

"Not like there aren't a lot of them there already," Lockwood laughed. "Maybe more around Boston than Los Angeles, but I'm pretty sure I can find some RedSox or Braves fans out west if I look hard enough. Not going to be more than one hundred people, I'm guessing. Plus immediate families, and we'll put them through some basic background checks, but I'm figuring that Gennadi already did that himself and has people he trusts."

"Excellent, General," Ingles replied. "Do you wish transport to town?"

"Had already been planning to sleep here tonight," Lockwood countered. "DC will need to digest all this and react, so I expect I'll see you or one of your people here in the morning."

"That, or I will telephone with updates," Ingles nodded. "Anything more than that?"

"Ask the Navy folks at the Pentagon to reach out to their friends in the Royal Navy," Lockwood said. "I want to know who those punks were that Sasha shot down. And where they came from. If that's the National Security Council or the Central Intelligence Agency, have someone ask them to get involved. Things like this don't just happen out of the blue. Past that, I'm circling until you radio me in."

"Very good, General. I'll start coding up telegrams as soon as I get back and will keep you apprised of the situation as it develops."

Lockwood watched the spy head to his car and depart. Used to be, all sorts of Army and Navy attaches got attached to embassies to do things, but this new CIA was leaning on putting their own people there, though the branches all had their own offices still. The Joint Chiefs of Staff kept the civilians on their side of the playground, but as he'd told Ingles, Sasha kinda went right down the middle.

Now he just needed to figure out how to update and employ the team using the CIA's money instead of his, even as the Joint Chiefs were going to continue to be deeply involved.

That, and what Sasha and the others could do about all the troublemakers out there.

CHAPTER 14

Sasha awoke at the knock, followed by Yefim sticking his head into the room.

"You are needed urgently," the man said simply, before disappearing.

Sasha didn't hear any aircraft or gunfire outside, so hopefully only political developments.

Urgent meant that he didn't pause to shower, but got dressed quickly and headed to the new command space Gennadi had taken over at one end of the commissary.

The Colonel handed him a newspaper as soon as Sasha walked up. The headline screamed trouble.

Part of it was the news of the N.A.T.O. formally coming into force today, but that was a known quantity, since the Americans and others had all formally approved the treaty in the spring.

It was the news from American President Truman that took Sasha's breath away. And the quote that started it off.

"We have evidence that within recent weeks an
atomic explosion occurred in the U.S.S.R."

Much other news and speculation followed, but Sasha could already feel the balance of the entire world shifting beneath his feet. Hopefully, for the better, but he could not tell for certain. The Americans and British appeared deeply surprised, the news generating shock and possibly anger in Washington and London both from details in the article.

Until yesterday, the Americans had maintained a monopoly on atomic weapons. The only nation to have them, having used two to annihilate Hiroshima and Nagasaki in 1945. The logic had been brutal, but understandable. To break the will of the Japanese people rather than forcing an Allied invasion that would have produced catastrophic casualties on both sides. Japan had been leveled and firebombed. And hit with atomic weapons twice, but they had already begun rebuilding. Had it been necessary to invade, that would have taken several years to complete, and cost millions of more lives.

And today, Stalin had the bomb.

Sasha more or less collapsed into a seat as he read, his legs unable to hold up his weight. As if by magic, a mug of coffee appeared in his hand and he let the heat attempt to break the ball of ice that had taken root in his belly.

It did not appear to be adequate to the task, but Sasha wasn't sure anything was.

He looked up at Gennadi and got a sober nod.

"What had been the original estimate in the West?" he asked, glancing around but Lockwood had not joined them yet.

"Another three to five years minimum," Gennadi replied calmly. "Obviously, everyone was wrong."

Sasha had to agree with that, but also obviously, he hadn't needed to know anything for his mission. Nor had Gennadi.

Yefim was hovering close, watching.

"Go wake General Carlyle," Sasha ordered. "He needs to know."

"Yes, sir."

Sasha paused and noted that all of them were automatically speaking in English these days. Even the Irish mechanics had learned it as a second language where necessary, though in their case they might see it as speaking American, a distinction which he understood.

Sasha poured more coffee down, but it still failed to warm him.

Lockwood appeared quickly, taking everything in. Sasha handed him the newspaper and sat back.

"Holy shit," Lockwood muttered as he worked through the article, finally looking up.

"I presume that you might need to contact the embassy as soon as possible," Sasha said simply. "And that everything we discussed yesterday might be put on hold. Or rescinded. Neither would offend me, as this news will need time to be digested."

"You said it," Lockwood agreed.

"Yefim, take the General to an office and make sure he is able to contact his people," Sasha said, locating the man. "I will take a shower, then return for breakfast and planning. Hopefully, he'll be able to join us at that time."

Sasha saw the two off, then shared a look with Gennadi.

"Is it better, or worse?" he asked.

"Top American generals, like Patton before he died or MacArthur more recently, have been loud about their opinion that the US should have kept going in 1945 and destroyed Moscow or Leningrad, preemptively starting that next World War that many felt was cut off too soon."

"We were all allies, at least of convenience, meeting at

Berlin," Sasha acknowledged. "I appreciate that nobody trusted each other, but it didn't have to turn out like this."

"It did not, but remember that Roosevelt died before the war ended," Gennadi replied. "And Atlee replaced Churchill, which probably did cause peace to break out, however fragile and brittle. Roosevelt was our ally, going back to the '30s when he tried to use trade to bring Stalin in from the cold. Churchill was and is a warmonger, first and foremost. One only has to look at his career over the last fifty years to see that."

"If we do cross that line and move to America, we might never be welcomed home, regardless of what might change," Sasha pointed out.

"I have already made my peace with such an outcome, Sasha," Gennadi replied. "And most of your people, hopefully all of them, will follow where you lead."

Sasha accepted that. He led the Red Branch, even as Gennadi was Red Branch Command.

But this morning, the world had changed.

It was his responsibility to make sure it was an improvement, because the Americans might panic at this moment, expecting that they would have to strike now, before Stalin was in a position to fight fire with fire.

And burn the whole world to the ground.

CHAPTER 15

Gennadi had comforted himself with the rest of the news as the two key players arranged the battlefield. Or the chess board.

Something.

In many ways, a Soviet atomic bomb probably was a stabilizing factor, because the Americans could not be immediate bullies to the rest of the world, as they often had been in Latin America.

The Berlin Blockade had always appeared to him as a stupid provocation, as it had allowed the Americans to stand the western German sectors up and given the Berliners themselves hope.

And he had expected it to devolve into open warfare at any of a number of points, but somehow it never had.

Gennadi assumed that someone on the Soviet side had been bluffing and been forced to back down ignobly when called on it.

But history was proving Churchill prescient. An Iron Curtain. Gennadi had seen it come into being and gain force in the three years since that speech.

Atomic bombs simply reinforced that everyone would have to behave or face annihilation.

And if no war could break out, then everything would have to remain in the shadows.

He wondered how prescient General Shuysky had been, when he had determined that the GRU needed something like the Red Branch, operating on the other side of those walls in order to hunt those war criminals that had escaped justice.

Sasha was not a spy. Nor, generally, was Gennadi. The former saw himself as a man trying to do the right thing, and had risen twice to thwart world-altering occasions that would have damaged American morale and possibly ignited a war. Gennadi would support him, even if it involved fighting other communists, or unrepentant fascists.

Whatever it took.

Sasha returned first. The kitchen took his order and then cooked it with care. Lockwood arrived about the time that Sasha finished eating, so they drank more coffee and waited.

"News?" Sasha asked in the uncomfortable silence that had descended.

"China had everyone distracted until yesterday," Lockwood replied quietly. "Mao finally kicked Chiang's ass across the straight to Formosa. Not sure if the fighting simmers down some there, or if the Mainlanders assemble a flotilla to invade and finish them off."

"Would the US Navy allow it?" Gennadi asked.

That had been the biggest thing in the news.

Until yesterday.

"Doubtful," Lockwood shrugged. "7th Fleet might station enough firepower in the Straits to make them all behave. Don't know if it would work, but Mao has a chore ahead of him, just getting the mainland in hand. That war's been going for nearly thirty years now, and a lot of folks might not support the communists just yet. At least the Berlin Airlift is finally done. And that without any shooting."

Gennadi noted the man's relief, and shared it.

Another war in Europe didn't do anybody any good. Now or tomorrow.

"What about Muroc?" Sasha asked.

"Messages have been sent to have everyone up their alert level there," Lockwood replied. "With updates about what happened here, so Zhidkov and Gradskaya know. And know why they shouldn't go anywhere. Lots of folks in Southern California are a lot more paranoid, so anyone trying that shit today might find themselves at the short end of a flight of Sabrejets in a hurry. Should be good."

Gennadi tried to share his enthusiasm but found it difficult. Everything felt like it was poised on the verge of an explosion, a fuse that had been lit but nobody knew how long it was, or where it would explode.

He drew Lockwood's eye.

"I expect a message from someone shortly," Gennadi said. "Either our landlord or the Irish government itself. An eviction, if you will, though I have no idea if they will give us days or months."

"My people have reached out to them," Lockwood replied. "Washington will be involved at some level, once everyone gets updated and this mess blows over. But I agree. You should pack."

"Difficult and possibly rude question for you then, Lockwood," Sasha broke in. "Is this situation serious enough that we would all be safer having our gear transported on an American warship instead of hiring a random freighter?"

Gennadi approved. They had a list of civilian captains that

Zinoviy had supplied. Trustworthy comrades all. Fully vetted. But asking the US Navy to get involved certainly would put Lockwood Carlyle on the spot to prove their interest.

"Lemme ask," the man nodded. "Possibly not the worst idea, since the Werewolf Legion has vanished at sea after it departed Sao Paulo. Granted, only six weeks ago, but they should have appeared somewhere that our people would have taken notice. Hoping that nobody sold them an old German U-boat or something."

"I presume that there are bounties on their heads now," Gennadi interjected. "One presumes that they would have made arrangements for greater secrecy. What I can't determine is who might hire them, if they have made enemies of the US Government."

"Same here," Lockwood replied. "More worried about who attacked us yesterday, and how we stop it and hunt them down."

Gennadi appreciated that the man saw the three of them on the same team. They generally were, because destroying the Werewolf Legion was high on everyone's list. It was everything else afterwards where things diverged.

At the same time, he agreed. Someone was after the Red Branch.

He needed to destroy them, too.

CHAPTER 16

"You failed," Taras growled at Colonel Matveev. "Worse, the American Air Force and Navy are both involved now from our agent reports. Visibly and officially. How long until those two prisoners are broken and tell the British the truth?"

Matveev shrugged carefully.

"Both men are GRU agents," he replied. "They have been in place since we inserted them after the war, with several years of hiding in western England. It is unfortunate that the Royal Navy picked them up instead of the Irish, but not terminal, as each cell is kept isolated from any other for exactly this reason. We do not believe that any other agents are at risk at present."

"And your spies inside the British government?" Taras pursued doggedly.

"Have not made any indication that the two men will be subject to anything but standard interrogation and probably incarceration, at least until we decided to get involved, possibly identifying them as ours and demanding a trade. Until then, they should be safe."

"And what will you do to get to Kryvenko, now that he is better protected?" Taras demanded.

"There are teams in Washington and Los Angeles that have been prepared for action," Matveev replied. "Direct action, since we could not bring in any sort of combat aircraft to threaten the Red Branch. Especially not as there are several Air Forces bases in the vicinity at both locations, keeping a very tight security of their experimental aircraft. Especially at the place called Muroc, where the rest of the team has been based since coming to the United States."

"That does not sound like they can be attacked," Taras noted.

"Not on the base, no," Colonel Matveev agreed. "They cannot stay there forever. And if we do not have nearly the number and quality of spies in the US government that we do the British, there is only Los Angeles as a major city nearby, with most of the other places in Southern California no more than outlying villages. Everything has to pass that way. Better, if they fly, we can track them. If they move on the ground, there is an undercover Spetsnatz team already equipped with motor-cycles of an American design, as well as American equipment."

"And how could such an assassination be covered up?" Taras asked derisively.

"Not all Americans follow the wholesome image that the movies project, General," Matveev said delicately. "There is an emerging, anti-social subculture based around gangs of hooli-gans on motorcycles. Much of it appears centered on smaller towns outside of Los Angeles along the very roads that Red Branch vehicles would have to take to get to the port itself. They can be violent, and appear to support themselves as crim-inal gangs."

"And the government does not crush them?" Taras asked, surprised.

"They do not have camps like Siberia, Comrade General,"

Matveev bowed his head. "Such men might face a certain period of incarceration, but even then it is mere months in a jail unless they have committed one of the most violent crimes."

"And they wonder why the Soviet Union is destined to replace them," Taras scoffed. "Still, you have failed, Colonel."

He watched the man pale. And remain silent, which was good. Taras was not in the mood for excuses.

"Since you warned them that they were threatened, you will travel to Los Angeles yourself, Colonel," Taras ordered. "There, you will personally supervise the team involved. I will not settle for less than the destruction of the Red Branch. Am I clear?"

Matveev gulped and nodded.

"Dismissed," Taras ordered.

He watched the man depart, still fuming but less so. Matveev would take the blame at this point, while Taras could claim the glory for the mission's success.

The General Staff had ordered Kryvenko's destruction.

It was coming.

CHAPTER 17

Sasha had been concerned when the enormous American bomber came in and landed. A Boeing B-50, itself a model radically upgraded from the wartime B-29 with better engines and other improvements that had been intended for the war, but the Japanese had surrendered before facing them.

These days, as he understood it, those craft were intended to fly to Moscow or other targets with atomic bombs, so they were heavily armed.

And it was huge, compared to the Camel he was used to. Not as fast but possessing a ferry range that would let it fly them to Washington, or even directly to Muroc near Los Angeles on a single tank of fuel.

No jet could do such a thing, though he had heard about new aerial refueling systems that were greatly improved from the primitive techniques before the war. What could he do if they could refuel without landing their jets?

Sasha wasn't sure, but he continued to appreciate that every year brought a new innovation in aviation, though he was concerned that it would hopefully slow down at some point.

He and Lockwood were suited up for flight with the crew

forward, the plane itself being a bomber rather than the more comfortable transport they had flown before. It was fully armed and the crew were serious about things, with all guns cleared as they took off.

Sasha and Lockwood rode in seats installed near the radio operator, giving the impression that this particular craft was used thus often enough to have spent the time.

"All will be well with Gennadi?" Sasha asked as the giant vulture took flight at the end of the runway.

"The Irish are on the alert to watch the place," Lockwood replied on the headset. "And an American cruiser has been dispatched to deliver some marines to help box things up, then carry the cargo to San Diego, while various Irish passengers who need to pack will come later via New York City."

Sasha nodded.

He was looking forward to the next steps but understood that things were going to be a bit nerve-wracking.

"Has your government changed its mind about hiring the Red Branch?" he pursued, cognizant that the rest of the crew could possibly listen in on the intercom as they spoke over the noise of the engines.

"Nobody has mentioned anything to me," Lockwood replied. "At the same time, they knew I was coming home and bringing you, so operational security might take precedence and we'll hear tomorrow. You rethinking your choices?"

Sasha considered the question. And his response.

On the one hand, vast new vistas of possibility with American money backing him. And presumably American intelligence.

On the other, limitations on things like slipping in and quietly assassinating some of those men who should have been hanged from the neck until dead.

Nuremberg had only gone after two dozen. As far as Sasha was concerned, having read the reports, they should have taken a hard look at every officer of Oberst rank or higher in the entire Wehrmacht, and every single officer and senior non-com with SS badges.

And hanged hundreds or even thousands of them for what they had done. Especially to the Jews and Roma.

Far too many had been allowed to slip the noose and pretend that they had been simple, honest soldiers, following orders that had sounded legitimate.

Thus does evil prosper.

But the Americans had insisted on second chances. Or simply kidnapping the important scientists and taking them home to design and improve the same systems for Truman that they had for Hitler.

"I am not rethinking, Lockwood," Sasha said after a moment's pause. "I am concerned, however, with what we might do. The Nightviper is not a naval aircraft, able to fly from the deck of a carrier on a mission. We are, instead, simply mercenaries, though I have a secondary mission of hunting down my enemies and seeing them destroyed. Since we don't think that was the Werewolf Legion, I have two such groups."

"Anybody bombing Ireland gets my dander up, Sasha," Lockwood replied. "Washington wants them hunted down, too. And we'll probably take the intelligence we find and turn it over to you to do something destructive with. That, and call your reporter buddy in Virginia with a scoop."

"Your superiors would allow such a story?"

Sasha was still astounded at the raw freedom the press enjoyed in the West, able to print nearly anything they wanted, and hardly suffering consequences later. So unlike his youth.

"They would," Lockwood grinned. "It makes great copy. It

will distract a lot of folks from losing China or the Ruskies having the bomb, because you are a hero and they can relate to that."

"Are we meeting him in Washington?" Sasha pressed.

"Planning to have someone fly him out to Muroc after you get settled," Lockwood countered. "That way, he can write vague hints about exciting new aircraft that the Red Branch and the Air Force are developing. Makes people feel safe in a dangerous world. If anything, you undersell your accomplishments there, Sasha."

"I was doing what was necessary to save the world," Sasha replied darkly.

"Not a lot of folks would have done that once," Lockwood pointed out. "You've already done it twice, and I expect more as time goes by. You have that heroic stature."

Sasha let that one go by without comment. He understood that Gennadi had seen it. Had hired him specifically for it, when Sasha would have happily remained a test pilot exploring new aircraft and technologies.

But someone had to save the world.

And someone else was trying to kill him for it, over and above Alois Voss.

He would need to return the favor.

PART TWO
MUROC

CHAPTER 18

Sasha was home. It was strange to think of the Muroc Air Base as home, but it was like the places in Russia where he had taken experimental aircraft aloft and tested them.

The people were the same, but for having different uniforms and accents. Test pilots and their ground crew were apparently the same the world over, and the locals here had accepted him and his people without question.

Washington had been a short stop, dropping off Lockwood with a promise that he would follow on, with Addison Walker possibly joining him, the latter after getting a stern talking-to by the Air Force folks.

Sasha was flying Red-4 today. Not that he needed to, but he would have a spare pilot soon. Gennadi had a list of candidates, but the review had been put on hold by the sudden move and all had been notified of the unexpected delay.

Nikon would have to break in a new flier, and the plane itself needed to be stretched and tested occasionally.

Sasha had told everyone the story. Vanya was utterly frigid with rage. Lyuba molten with fury. The rest had gotten a hard look in their eyes promising to unleash the hounds of hell, the next time something untoward happened.

"Nikon, how is our perimeter?" Sasha asked on the internal line.

"Two teams of armed Sabrejets on patrol, Commander," Nikon replied without looking up from his radar screen. "East and west of us, with ground air defense stations on alert."

Muroc's senior people had taken the lessons of Red Branch Command to heart as well, and kept aloft patrols whenever a Nightviper was about to fly. Ground radar was challenging every signal that appeared.

He felt safe. Safe enough. Red-4 was also armed, but he was not doing anything more than keeping in practice. He and Nikon, who was still a little bit of an orphan, without his pilot partner that made a team.

Still, Sasha picked out a few rock formations and practiced strafing and bombing runs. Rockets were not a thing he had used much in the past, but he understood the theory, so he added a couple of practice low-level rocket passes as well, wondering if they could acquire the necessary weapons from Lockwood's people, or needed to find them elsewhere. And how much work it would be to adapt the Nightviper, or if they should see about that theoretical *next aircraft* various people were talking about.

Time would tell.

"Red-1, this is Red-Base," Yuri's voice abruptly came over the radio. "You have a visitor at the strip. Suggest you cut this flight short and rejoin us soonest."

Odd. Vague and obscure, which was unlike Yuri, so probably someone quite important, though he had no idea who that might be. Lockwood was supposed to be arriving tomorrow at the earliest, and no massive B-50s had appeared from the East Coast.

Still, he brought the nimble craft around and located the runway in his mind, lining it up already for a downwind pass.

"Red-1, returning to base, requesting clearance of the runway to land," he said formally.

"Red-1, you are clear for approach," a man replied. Muroc Tower, keeping watch on everything and everyone. "We have you on radar. Five minutes out. See you shortly."

"Thank you, Muroc Tower," Sasha replied. "Five minutes."

Who had come?

CHAPTER 19

Lyuba had no idea who the man was, but the locals all treated him with a great deference bordering on idol worship, so she watched and listened.

Tall and somewhat heavyset, but more bulky than fat. Dark hair slicked back from a side part and combed over. Double-breasted suit of impeccable tailoring.

He had taken notice of her, then nodded at some internal conversation and largely ignored her after that, so he was not one of those men led astray by their lusts.

In the distance, Sasha was about to land, gear down and approaching with the delicate-but-firm touch she expected from him in all things. Lyuba exited the building two steps behind the stranger and just ahead of Vanya and several others, following the man to the runway apron where Sasha was bringing Red-4 into line with the others.

Yuri was up in the tower, and would join them presently, but she wanted to see how this man reacted to Sasha.

You could tell a great deal about someone from that alone. In Washington, it had let her split that first large meeting of scientists and generals into the smart ones and the political hacks who would have been commissars or senior Party members back home.

Red-4 came to rest and powered down. The ground crew swarmed expertly, American airmen who had seemingly taken great joy in the Nightviper and the Red Branch.

Sasha and Nikon emerged and the stranger walked right up to *Cernunnos*.

"That is not a Ghost 103 powering you," the man said emphatically. "Sound's too low and too loud. What the hell did you put in there?"

Sasha sized the man up. Noted that she and Vanya had moved to the points of a triangle with the stranger bracketed on all sides, but he was not a threat.

He struck her as an aeronautical engineer. Like her. And a sharp one, if he knew engine sounds that well.

"It has been upgraded from the Rolls-Royce Nene by Klimov, back in the Soviet Union," Sasha replied neutrally. "We were able to smuggle out designs and our first engines when we also got pilots and flight crews. Since then, the factory in Ireland has been able to quietly reproduce parts."

"How's it stack up against the GE J47 in the F-86?" the man immediately pressed on.

"Roughly comparable for thrust," Sasha said. "I haven't seen the maintenance records to know how they stand for durability, but our engines are a bit more mature, I think. And the Nightviper is far lighter than the Sabrejet, so better maneuverability in many situations and straightline level speed, though we cannot approach Mach with straight wings. I would expect to lose a wing or my tail if we dove that hard, while the Sabre can do it."

The stranger surprised her by turning to look at Lyuba finally. Appraising her carefully.

"They tell me you're the aircraft designer brains around here," he said simply. "We'll need to go pretty deep into some of your details."

Lyuba simply nodded at the man, a bit breath-taken by his abruptness, but there was nothing sexist to it. Not like most American government people she'd met.

Simply an impatience to get things done in the shortest time possible, without a lot of time for other bureaucratic intrusions.

He turned back to Sasha.

"Lockwood Carlyle asked me to meet you folks and talk aircraft," he said. "He's in the air now, and will be here in a few hours, but I got questions, and he can't answer them, so I flew out direct to ask."

Sasha nodded.

"And you would be?" Sasha asked politely.

"Huh? Oh, right," the man seemed taken aback, then shook himself and smiled, holding out a hand to shake. "Kelly Johnson. Lockheed. I design aircraft."

Lyuba was both surprised and impressed. She knew that name. The American P-38 Lightning that had been so effective in the Pacific War had been his design. As had others.

And he was here because Carlyle had requested it?

She could hardly wait.

CHAPTER 20

Sasha caught his gasp silently and shook the man's hand.

Kelly Johnson was famous in certain circles. Possibly the best aeronautical engineer and aircraft designer alive, including all those folks back home who had their own design bureaus.

All of them, regardless of their own pedestals, stood below Johnson.

The Red Branch had enveloped the man, but there was no hostility to it.

"Coffee?" Sasha suggested, gesturing to the main building.

If Lockwood was coming, there might be things to cover before then. And how often did you get to talk to a genius at the top of his game?

"Yeah," Johnson nodded, immediately turning and blowing through the group like an icebreaker in polar waters.

Sasha fell in on his wing, and the rest were like geese headed south.

Coffee. Afternoon pastries, warm, so someone in the kitchen had been planning ahead. And knew his craft, because cinnamon rolls were nothing Sasha had understood until he had come here.

To the wealth of America, that cinnamon was so common that it was used to make rolls for everyday people. It was like that first diner that John the farmer had taken him after he landed in Virginia.

Abundance almost beyond imagination. What might the Soviet Union have been able to accomplish, had the rest of the world left them alone instead of invading in 1920 and meddling again and again?

He savored the gooiness of the roll with a twinge of guilt.

"That aircraft started on a design board as a de Havilland Vampire," Johnson began as soon as everyone got settled; him, Lyuba, and Vanya at the table, and the rest around the room listening. "And the Venom is starting to fly, but you're past that already. What else have you done?"

Sasha was taken aback by the man's intensity, but it was not hostile. A bottomless well of curiosity, perhaps.

And they were in the middle of Muroc, perhaps the second or third most carefully guarded site in North America, behind the Pentagon and Fort Knox where all the gold was supposedly protected.

Plus, Lockwood had sent for the man.

"We have access to certain designs that de Havilland and Vickers have both wanted to build, but the British lacked the funds," Sasha offered a touch obliquely.

Suggesting spies without mentioning whose.

"Gotcha," Johnson agreed. "Old tech, though, since they started flying those in '43 and got introduced to the RAF formally in '46. You've upgraded them significantly from those."

"Yes," Sasha said simply. "But I have spoken with Lockwood and others and everyone agrees that the first models of the new F-86 are at least as good as the Nightviper, and will only get better as people refine things."

"Better believe that," Johnson said. "I've been working on a new design for the Air Force's Penetration Fighter program, but I don't think it's going to work out, because we built it more rugged than we needed, and the engines that I was promised have never been completed, so the craft is kind of a dog. Those Westinghouse J34s are just crap."

Sasha took the man's word for it. Johnson was legendary in the industry for his ability to instinctively and intuitively find the perfect right answer, entirely off the cuff, offering probabilities and predictions that might take months of laborious calculation to verify. And supposedly, he was never more than a few percent off in his guesses.

Except that could you really call them guesses when he seemed to be always right?

Sasha didn't know.

"What are you designing, if you are allowed to discuss it?" Sasha asked delicately.

"XF-90," Johnson said. "Heavy, like I said. Maybe overbuilt. Durable enough to take 12g's because nobody really understands what happens out there beyond Mach One. I expect it will be old hat in a couple of years, but we gotta get through those years first."

"And your engines are insufficient?" Lyuba asked.

Johnson turned to look at her and nod.

"Too little thrust," he replied. "That was why I was interested in what this Klimov team had. Or whatever else we might be able to borrow or steal."

"What's it fly like?" she asked.

Sasha contained his smile. This was not the tone or body language of a beautiful woman prompting a man to blather, but two aeronautical engineers about to dive headlong into a technical conversation that Sasha might be the only other person in here able to understand.

No, Junior Sergeant Dmitri Yefimov and Yuri had joined them at some point. Dmitri was a mechanical genius, but not a designer. Still, he could likely follow things, though he sat off to one side pretending ignorance for now.

He might pounce later, depending.

"It's got the intake and low-wing layout of the old P-80 Shooting Star we built, but with a 35 degree sweep-back on the wings, plus a sharply-pointed nose, wingtip tanks, and those two Westinghouse J34-WE-11 axial-flow turbojet engines that just won't give me what I need."

Lyuba gave him a meaningful glance, so Sasha leaned in.

"Would the Air Force let you put in alternate engines?" he asked. "Foreign built, perhaps?"

Johnson got cagey and sharp.

"Like?" he asked in a tone that only sounded innocent on the surface.

"Gennadi Nazarenko, who is Red Branch Command in Ireland, though they might be moving closer depending on Washington, has access and inroads to British designs," Sasha offered carefully. "I have heard impressive things about the new Armstrong Siddeley Sapphire ASSa.2. A little short of double the thrust of the Ghost 103. Perhaps a quarter or so better than the GE J47 in the Sabrejet."

Johnson's eyes had gotten big, then closed to almost slits.

"The Air Force would probably never allow it," the man replied carefully. "And I'm fifty/fifty that a Soviet a-bomb causes everyone to rethink the whole Penetration Fighter plan entirely, because it was more of a dogfighter for air superiority, and the new Lockheed P-94 doesn't even have guns. Carry a wallop of unguided rockets in launcher pods instead, on the logic that you want to blast through a squadron of bombers and hit everything at once as you go by."

"That strikes me as a touch random in execution," Lyuba offered neutrally.

"Their money," Johnson shrugged. "I can argue with them, but they've got the checkbook at the end of the day. Same time, Carlyle tells me that you aren't going to be working for the Air Force anyway. Is he correct?"

It was Sasha's turn to shrug back.

"There have been suggestions of civilian money," he replied. "Quietly hunting down certain criminal elements and such. And we're international, so we should have a great deal more leeway for that sort of thing."

"Huh," Johnson said. "Then the XF-90 might be adaptable, depending on the size of the Armstrong Siddeley."

He reached into an inside pocket of his blazer and brought out a small notebook. As Sasha watched, the man did a quick sketch of the Nightviper, apparently from memory, that still almost looked like a technical line drawing from Gennadi's safe.

"This is your craft," he said, then paused and drew an arrow-shaped craft with a tail and swept wings with tanks on the tips below it. "This is the XF-90. The air intakes are behind the cockpit a bit, leading back to dual engines. Your aircraft are all configured as night-fighters, though."

"Radar operator and navigator position, yes," Lyuba replied. "And night operations for all-weather strike as well as intercept capabilities, instead of having a different aircraft for each mode of combat like most people did it during the war and more recently."

"Gotcha," Johnson said. "Let's assume the engines are close

enough to keep the same general lines aft. Rebuild for a side-by-side cockpit like you have now?"

"Tandem for better aerodymamics," Lyuba corrected him. "With the nose rebuilt for a radar system operated from the back seat. And guns instead of rockets. What did you plan?"

Johnson seemed surprised, but immediately nodded and leaned in himself.

"We designed ports for six 20mm cannons under the air intakes here, but they haven't been fitted," he said.

"What about the new English 30 mm ADEN revolver cannon in a removable gun pack that the British are starting to insist on?" she pressed. "Four of them should be about the same space. Better killing power at melee ranges. The F-86 right now only has 12.7mm machine guns, but I do not think that those will be sufficient to engage modern aircraft."

"Especially not the 90," Johnson laughed. "We built that thing tough."

"Exactly," Lyuba agreed. "I would prefer killing power over throwing a lot of bullets that perhaps bounce off my target."

"How good are you?" Johnson asked bluntly, then looked around at the rest of them.

"46th Guards Night Bomber Aviation Regiment," she replied evenly. "*The Night Witches.*"

Johnson whistled, then started a third sketch.

Sasha looked around at the room and nodded.

"Dismissed," he said. "We'll be a while."

The rest nodded and began to filter out. No reason to keep them all here. He stayed. Vanya smiled and joined Yuri in departing.

Quickly it was down to him, Lyuba, and Kelly Johnson. And that man's sketchbook.

What could they come up with?

CHAPTER 21

Lockwood had been warned by Captain Zhidkov that Sasha and *Banshee* had been in the commissary with Kelly for several hours by the time he'd landed.

On the one hand, it was somewhat frightening what those three might have accomplished, lacking the sorts of adult supervision that Kelly occasionally needed when it was necessary to impress and beguile Senators with their hands on the purse strings.

On the other, while in Washington he'd had a chance to meet with a few folks at the newly reconfigured Central Intelligence Agency and gotten their go-ahead to consider using some black funds to do things.

Worse, *Banshee* had been the one that had impressed the shit out of all of those old dogs, and done it with her calm mind and expertise at that damned rocket plane. That, and the few of them who actually understood what the term *Night Witch* **entailed**.

Lockwood entered via the kitchen, grabbing a roll and coffee before slipping in the back way to where the three potential troublemakers were all heads-down on a sheet of paper, with Kelly holding the pen. For good or ill.

Had the future of aviation already been created in this room? It was Kelly. And a blank slate. And an open checkbook.

Frightening only began to describe that situation.

Kelly looked up at his entrance and Lockwood felt the impact of that intellect lock on like a radar installation.

"Penetration Fighter program is already out the window, isn't it?" Kelly asked as Lockwood moved close and took the chair next to Sasha.

Lockwood considered his response. And things classified at extremely high levels that he had been briefed about in Washington. Stalin had everybody wound up.

"I would not be entirely surprised, no," Lockwood equivocated carefully. "Instead of leading bombers in to clear the skies of Soviet defenders, we might be looking at an emphasis on Interceptor aircraft capable of rapidly locating and engaging Soviet bombers on the defense."

Kelly nodded.

"I'm going to assume that the XF-90 won't be picked, because of the engine issue that's not your fault or ours," Kelly said bluntly. Like always. "Then the whole program will be scrapped without ever buying anything, at least for a couple of years. You're still going to need a jet-powered night-fighter soon, because the Black Widow and the Twin Mustang won't cut it for much longer."

Lockwood nodded without comment. There was a reason he regularly talked to Kelly. And listened to the man. Usually right. Scarily right, most of the time, too.

"New radar systems will make it possible for the pilot to handle things alone," Lockwood offered, mostly to see where Kelly went with it.

"Maybe, but once you have multiple guided missiles going back and forth in the sky, I'm betting you're back to somebody handling all that while the other woman flies the plane. Plus whatever defensive systems you'll come up with stop missiles from tracking you. Gonna be a mess."

Lockwood silently noted the gender and presumed that *Banshee* had worked her charm on the man.

Most of the folks in Washington *still* underestimated her intelligence. Badly.

"What have you considered?" Lockwood asked the group, dreading leaving these three alone with such an open-ended question.

"Kelly suggested taking the nose of the new F-94 and mating it with the wings and rear of the XF-90," Sasha replied first. "That's radar up front, plus a tandem cockpit. Guns have space in back already. Engines were the problem."

Lockwood really didn't like the way the other two were smiling. No good would come of it, but at least whatever it was would be aimed at someone else. Like those Germans Sasha was so angry at. Even worse than the Joint Chiefs, which took some doing.

"Oh?"

"Can we ask the Brits to sell us a couple dozen Armstrong Siddeley engines and an ongoing parts program?" Kelly asked. "I don't have time for them to license Westinghouse or somebody to come up with something and build a new plant. That'd take years and Sasha and Lyuba don't have that kind of time."

Lockwood wracked his brain to remember what AS had built most recently, but then he remembered hints that Nazarenko had connections into British Intelligence and possibly the Atlee Government.

"The flight testing of the XF-90 was a disappointment," Lockwood offered.

"Engines too weak to do the job, because the latest generation still isn't ready," Kelly snapped. "I can adjust the design of the frame to make it a lot lighter, but that's not going to gain me enough weight savings for those engines. I'd rather have the power to make this design go fast while being tough enough to dogfight at Mach and still bomb folks."

Lockwood turned to *Banshee*, noting the deadly gleam in her eyes. Yes, high-speed, low-level bombing. Gennadi and Sasha had both mentioned that she was the unquestioned expert there, even as she was supposedly as good a dogfighter as anybody they'd sent up against her here at Muroc.

"Air Force would never go for it," he said, holding up a hand to stop these three from jumping down his throat. "They aren't funding this. Central Intelligence is. They gave me a little bit of *carte blanche* to do things, but this pushes even that envelope a little, so I'll need something definitive I can put in front of them to get funds transferred."

Kelly's eyes lit up in that way that they did. The other two were almost as bad.

"You want formal calculation charts run for everything?" Kelly asked. "Or just an estimate from me on costs to adapt the engines, steal the nose sections I need from the F-94 assembly line, and get some guns from the Brits?"

"What did you do?" Lockwood countered carefully.

Dread took hold.

"Turned the XF-90 into a strategic fighter," Kelly grinned. "Night duties, ground attack, air superiority, penetration. The works. Expensive, and capable, but I don't figure we're building more than a dozen of them initially, plus parts, unless you decide to give Sasha command of an entire air wing to do things, which might not be the dumbest idea I've ever heard."

"How?"

"Adding aerial refueling capabilities from a probe-and-drogue in the nose section where the F-94's guns would have gone," *Banshee* added. "We'd like to discuss acquiring a tanker, but the Camel can be outfitted with pods under the wings to handle that for now."

Lockwood processed all that, then put the results under Sasha's command in his head.

Washington might even go for it, because one of Northrop's flying wings had flown out of here over the last few years, though number two had crashed and killed the whole crew in the summer of 1948. The other plane still worked, but it had looked to Kelly like those contracts weren't going anywhere. Same as Kelly was probably right about the Penetration Fighter program.

He usually was, when he expressed an opinion.

Folks had made it to South America and quietly looked at the remains of the Werewolf Legion Flying Wing. Plus confirmed the launch site of the Silver Eagle and interviewed Paraguayan military people who were quite happy that they hadn't accidentally gotten themselves invaded or bombed, depending on how pissed Truman and the Joint Chiefs would have been had Voss succeeded.

In light of all that, even them being ex-Soviet didn't really ruffle feathers, because he could spin that as White Russian and a lot of politicians would nod.

"Get me within ten percent," Lockwood told Kelly. "I can figure a way to sell that to the accountants on your rep. Later, have a couple of your people run formal numbers so I can file those for complaints next year, but the Nightviper's time is almost done."

And just in a few hours, Kelly, Sasha, and *Banshee* had apparently invented the future, after all.

Where would it take them?

CHAPTER 22

It had been a month of waiting, but the day had arrived. They were in a safe hangar this morning, not in formation because Sasha wasn't a martinet that needed to have his troops spit and polished so he could scream at them.

Instead, everyone was loaded up as if going on a mission. Officers had their Shanxi Type 17 pistols in holsters. Everyone but Arkadi had Thompsons slung, but nobody had a magazine inserted, instead carrying a satchel over one shoulder with three loaded magazines ready for use.

From there, specialist equipment as needed, with Ilya carrying a second bag of explosives and supplies. Nikon had his rochin and a few other Chinese weapons. Yanina, her medical kit. Vanya, a radio like Yuri's.

Somewhere—and Sasha carefully did not ask where—Oleg had acquired what he called a disguise kit, with various things like false facial hair, dye, and a few changes of clothing that would let him transform into different people as needed. Presumably, Oleg had charmed the locals enough that someone here knew someone working in Hollywood, not all that far away, and had gotten the bag for him.

Not asking seemed the wisest course, because he knew that Oleg had a reputation for insubordination, but the finer details revealed an entertainer who wanted to please people, living in a military were commissars had no sense of humor whatsoever, Vanya seemingly excluded.

It was a good team. Solid. Dependable.

Capable.

He would have to start interviewing a replacement pilot for Pavel soon, as well as finding people that could expand what the Red Branch could do on the ground. And keep their mouths shut about any other things that the US government might not sanction.

Like killing escaped Nazi war criminals who had reveled in their evil during the war years and then vanished into the shadows.

It would be a tightrope. He would manage. And perhaps rearrange his four radar operators to fly with new pilots at some point to help get them trained and comfortable with how the Red Branch did things.

It had been a whirlwind of a month. Kelly had called regularly, but mostly to get technical with Lyuba more than anything, conversations that didn't usually last as long as it took to find her and walk to the telephone. The Lockheed Corporation was apparently doing something in a facility so secure that Sasha was only allowed to know that such a thing existed, and no more.

Lockwood was spending time shuttling between Los Angeles proper, Washington, and Muroc, though they were apparently about to rename this base after Glen Edwards, a test pilot and Great Patriotic War hero who had been killed when that second Northrop YB-49 Flying Wing broke apart during a flight last year, killing everyone aboard.

Fitting, to name this place after a test pilot. One of the least safe jobs in the air, but utterly necessary. And Edwards had been awarded four Distinguished Flying Crosses and six Air Medals in his service.

Sasha was sad that he'd never gotten a chance to meet the man, because Edwards was impressive as hell on paper. And folks around here had good things to say about him.

But they were getting close to the next phase of life. Gennadi's cruiser transport had arrived at the US Navy base in San Diego. Lockwood had provided them another Commando aircraft today to haul the team to San Diego, where they would ride home in a convoy of trucks carrying the smaller gear, with the boxed up aircraft to be hauled on railcars and assembled later for flight.

Red Branch Command would be back in business. Sasha wouldn't say that having secret American funding was a chore, but the last month had been restricted mainly to flying F-86 and F-94 aircraft, both as testing for pilot certification, as well as to offer vague hints to Kelly and others about what the new MiG-15 might be like if they were ever encountered.

He could only get close, as he'd been gone long enough to not know what refinements Mikoyan and Gurevich had added for the production models from the early test prototypes.

And Sasha couldn't imagine what kind of conflict that would be, unless Stalin sent a force to China to help Mao at the same time the Americans sent a counter to Formosa to protect the now-homeless Nationalist government. For the moment, the US Navy was keeping aircraft carriers and fleet elements in the vicinity, mostly to force everyone to remain at arm's length.

Hopefully, that war could calm down and possibly allow some peaceful resolution, such as the Berlin Airlift had done.

Kelly promised the first new F-90 soon, apparently keeping

his teams working crazy hours, singing and laughing as they assembled it, if the rumors were to be believed. Except that it would not be an American plane, so that number was inappropriate.

Vanya had suggested calling the aircraft *Strix*, like the Vampire had become the *Nightviper*, and the name had stuck.

In the mythology of classical antiquity, a strix was a bird of ill omen, the product of magical metamorphosis that fed on human flesh and blood. Scientifically, also a breed of large, earless wood-owls, which fit perfectly as a night-fighter.

Because the Red Branch would be coming for you at night, as well.

Sasha studied the assembled group. Noted that the C-46 in the hangar with them had a distinctly civilian crew, in spite of landing here and being directed to fly to another military base down south shortly.

The Copilot appeared to be in charge. A Chinese woman named Chao Yan Ni who had introduced herself, then pointed to the pilot as her husband, a rumpled, English-looking American named Reuben Granger who had merely smiled and waved.

And the crew chief, responsible for getting Sasha, his people, and their gear loaded, was a tiny European woman named Tess Abbink. Barely came up to Sasha's shoulder. Fussy and precise.

"We're ready to load," he told Tess and Yan Ni finally.

"Officers up front," Tess replied. "Rest of you fill in behind that."

"Normally, we organize by flight crews," Vanya offered, then cringed back at little at her scowl.

"Not today," Tess said simply. "Load."

Discretion seemed the better part of valor, so Sasha

followed the woman in. Ended up front right next to Vanya, with Lyuba and Yuri across the aisle, probably laterally balanced pretty closely by overall mass, upon reflection.

The rest found their places and Yan Ni got the engines going as Tess got things put in place, scowling at the amount of firepower on display, but Sasha hadn't brought cases for the Thompsons and the aircraft had no racks to hold them.

Everyone ended up with theirs upright between their knees as they buckled in. Tess had smiled that nobody had them loaded. The pistols didn't count. Nor would he have listened to an order to disarm them.

Reuben came aft and leaned in to yell over the noise of the propellers.

"We're being escorted by combat aircraft?" he asked. "I mean, they said that before, but I didn't think they were serious."

"I got bombed and strafed at my base in Ireland a month ago," Sasha yelled back. "Shot him down afterwards, but you don't have guns here, do you?"

"Don't," Reuben nodded. "I'll tell the boss."

He turned and went back into the cockpit. Yan Ni turned to look over her shoulder, but didn't say anything. Merely shrugged and went back to work.

Lockwood had ordered a squadron of F-86 Sabrejets into the air as a training exercise today.

Armed.

Hopefully, they wouldn't be needed, but this was the entire Red Branch, minus only Gennadi, down at the base waiting for them.

And whatever else might come up.

CHAPTER 23

CHAPTER

Gennadi was glad to be on dry land again. The USS Macon was a lovely ship, and the officers had been quite charming, but Gennadi was not one for rough seas. Or even calm waters, generally.

Give him unmoving earth or clear skies any day.

But he was on land again.

Everything had been done under strictest secrecy, so he had come to California alone, while Yefim had sailed to New York City aboard a passenger liner with that group of Irish mechanics that would be joining him shortly via train, while others had discussions with their families about uprooting and moving away.

Apparently, Ireland sent a significant portion of its youth to America every year, so the ones he had originally been able to hire had been the ones mostly interested in staying home, though he had a list of contacts for adventurous siblings and cousins that he might want to hire here, already generally vetted by people he had himself vetted.

San Diego itself had too much sun. At least it was only warm, and not that cloying heat that grabbed Moscow in a death grip every summer. Cool breezes off the water suggested that this city might be a paradise.

If you liked that much sun.

Gennadi preferred gray, slightly drizzly, and sixteen degrees. Good weather for a jacket, without needing a wool long-coat in Leningrad winters. He had, at least, listened to the folks who suggested he carry his lightest fabric suits, while packing the heavy wools for later.

Gennadi could only imagine broiling today. Worse broiling. Something.

A sailor approached. Uniform suggested a Lieutenant. Clean cut. American boy. Earnest, as so many of them had been.

Gennadi might have suggested British Intelligence connections to these folks as well. That lie had worked well on General Carlyle, and the British tended to be closed-mouthed enough to not say anything to any strangers asking.

He understood that the British generally meant well, as long as you were pale skinned, but they truly did not understand how rough and dangerous the world might really be. Nor how many people in their colonies would be happy to see their backs. Or their blood.

And he was only taking a little advantage of them, because his mission was aimed at enemies of all civilization.

"Sir, your transport force has arrived at the base gates," the young, earnest Lieutenant said, snapping off a salute that was likely entirely inappropriate to a civilian, but Gennadi did not correct him.

Yet more confusion, if someone ever did try to dig.

"Lead on," Gennadi replied, smiling even, because it was a beautiful day, and he was living in America.

At least until someone discovered that he was a spy—of sorts—and things got ugly.

Double lives, and all that.

The Lieutenant took him back from the waterfront overlooking all that naval power, and into an office building that was attached to the warehouse where all of his crates and larger containers would eventually be hauled. At least nothing larger than several Nightvipers, wings removed for travel.

Hauling another camouflaged Ilyushin Il-28 bomber would have been complicated and painful. Unnecessary, as the one had ferried up from South America earlier this year.

"Coffee, sir?" the Naval Attache asked.

Gennadi presumed that the young man would fulfill the same role. A spy, but politely in uniform about it. Not digging, but watching.

"Yes," Gennadi replied. "Please. With cream and sugar."

Utter decadence, having coffee that wasn't as bitter and black as Russian winters. Gennadi could see how Pavel Zaslavsky had been seduced.

Sasha and Vanya had held the others true, so Gennadi could indulge himself occasionally. Or ask Sasha to be stern with him later.

So he sat, and sipped, and watched the polite spy watch him, no words passing. Gennadi was used to long flights in aircraft that hadn't had radios in those days, so you were alone with your own thoughts as long as you were in the air. It taught more patience than even Russian winters did.

Eventually, the Red Branch arrived. Gennadi was merely Red Branch Command, the administration of the thing.

Sasha as *Cernunnos. Banshee, Ecne,* and *Dunatis*—Lyuba, Vanya, and Yuri—who supported him. The men and women that supported them. Brigadier Carlyle had not come with them. Nor had the American designer who would be busy building new planes.

Gennadi had not gotten a straight answer yet about technology transfers. Things that might accidentally be stolen from his vaults by Soviet spies to send home later.

He would cross that bridge when he got there.

"The trip was uneventful?" Sasha asked as everyone got coffee, tea, or even soda pops from a refrigerator.

Utterest decadence. But that same wealth had given Stalin the guns, tanks, and aircraft that had defeated the Nazis. Stalin's equivalent wealth had been blood. It had been enough.

Barely.

"I am glad to be ashore," Gennadi replied diplomatically. "Everything has been unloaded and readied. The smaller boxes we will carry, while the larger containers will be sent up by rail shortly. Do we really need the entire team as escorts?"

Sasha noted the spy, otherwise still and silent as a gargoyle, before he spoke.

"We do not know who blew up your office in Dublin," Sasha replied. "Nor what they might be able to do here. Muroc is secured with many American soldiers. There are all the roads between here and there that concern me."

"You did not ask for a military escort?" Gennadi asked, noting that everyone was armed, with submachine guns slung on backs.

"We are not working for the US military," Sasha replied, no doubt speaking for the Attache to hear. "They have done us some favors, but there are still limits. Plus, we wanted this operation to be low profile, like turning off your motors and gliding at low altitude to bomb your target."

Lyuba Gradskaya. Night Witch.

"Such activities are risky," Gennadi reminded him.

Casualties among the 558th and 46th Guards had been horrendous.

Necessary.

Brutal, nonetheless.

Sasha nodded.

"Five trucks, as I understand it," he said. "Five officers with you, Gennadi. A half day driving and we will be back to Muroc, then we can figure out what Kelly and Lockwood will allow, going forward."

Gennadi noted that he was on first name basis with both important players, but Sasha had the commanding presence and charm to manage. And Lyuba had the brains to stand the sexist Americans off. The Soviet Union wasn't always advanced that way, but still far better than the West, in terms of liberating the genders.

"All of you are armed," Gennadi noted. "Heavily, I might add."

"And this is for you," Sasha said, removing his Thompson and ammunition pouch from his shoulder and resting them on the table.

The poor Lieutenant's eyes nearly bugged out of his head as Gennadi claimed the weapons and nodded.

He might not be as deadly as the others, but Gennadi knew how to use such weapons.

He had only been shot down that one time at the end, but every pilot had been prepared for such a day to arrive.

Hopefully, that was not today.

PART THREE
SAN BERNARDINO COUNTY

CHAPTER 24

Yuri rode in the lead truck at Sasha's command, when he might have been more comfortable in the last one. Vanya and Arkadi had that duty. Colonel Nazarenko was second, then Sasha, then Lyuba.

One officer for each cab. One or more crew member in back, along with American marines who had pistols, helmets, and arm bands suggesting that they were military police. One driving, one riding in back.

Being the navy, Yuri presumed that Shore Patrol mostly broke up bar fights. He had known many sailors in his time.

The inland desert north of the mountains was hot. Had been all summer, and was only now starting to cool as autumn set in. The coast, however, had been lovely.

If he wasn't Red Branch, Yuri could see retiring to such a place, as, apparently, a great many former sailors did. It was, after all, the American Dream.

He had his radio beside him on the seat as another Shore Patrol marine drove the truck. Yuri wondered if they were being escorted, protected, or hauled off to a hot, Siberian work camp.

The Americans were friendly enough, but there was an air of reticence today. Or Marines were naturally surly people. Hard to tell.

The roads were generally clear. No great highways, so they were following smaller roads from town to town, frequently parallel to railroad beds. Yuri wasn't sure why they were hauling things via truck instead of train, other than it had let them spend lunchtime on a navy base, talking and being seen in their pretty, blue uniforms that stood out.

Especially Lyuba and Yanina, who had mostly sniffed at American sailors. Lyuba was a beauty that would stop traffic anywhere. Yanina was built like a Russian peasant, broad and square. Stolid as well as solid.

And armed, which had caused everyone pause.

Sasha, no doubt, impressing the Americans with a civilian mercenary air company, operating with American assistance. Off to save the world again soon, presumably.

He had still not seen anything that would be an improvement on his Camel. Even the secret British designs for the English Electric EE.A1 that had supposedly flown a few months ago suggested that it would merely be as good.

Not better.

And the jet engines were not developed enough to make a proper heavy bomber efficient yet. He had seen the new Boeing C-97 Stratofreighter, both for cargo and as an aerial tanker. Big, yes, but slow. Lumbering beasts. Camels, certainly, but the dumb kind that carried lots of boxes.

Not the pretty ones you raced across the sands.

His radio chirped.

"Red-Base," Yuri replied.

"Red-2," Vanya said. "We are being followed by many men on motorcycles. Organized, rather than a group out for a ride."

"What colors are they wearing," the marine driving suddenly looked over at Yuri with an intense scowl.

"What?"

"Black leather jackets with some sort of logo or design on the back," the man continued. "Possibly a vest in a bright color. What color?"

He had keyed the microphone as the man spoke, so Vanya heard all that.

"Color?" Vanya asked. "The color is trouble. I see guns coming out. Alert everyone that we are being attacked."

CHAPTER 25

Colonel Kazimir Matveev was not entirely comfortable on an American motorcycle, but he had trained on similar equipment for this mission. And had had a few weeks to practice while waiting for the traitors to emerge from the safety of the American base up north.

Captain Ippolit Yegorov had been inserted as part of the demobilization of American troops after the war, a GRU strike team that also appeared as a motorcycle gang on the safe side of illegality. Loud and boisterous, but not criminals requiring that they be arrested and perhaps unmasked by the American authorities.

Someone had been planning for the day when Soviet troops would have to invade the American mainland, possibly via Alaska and Canada, though Kaz had no idea what sorts of teams might have been inserted into Anchorage, Vancouver, or Seattle.

Need to know, and he didn't. He only needed to know the Los Angeles chapter, as they called themselves.

Trouble. Today, the trouble would get even worse, as they

were all armed with American weapons, on American bikes, with American papers.

And a traitorous legion as their targets.

Captain Yegorov had had them waiting at a roadside diner, drinking and eating like normal citizens as he had awaited a phone call from San Diego. Then piss breaks inside and preparations behind the building, getting the loud machines ready and rumbling.

Five trucks had driven past in a convoy. Nearly identical to the Studebaker US6 2½-ton 6×6 tactical trucks he had driven during the war, manufactured and exported in vast numbers by the Americans.

Kaz didn't know which one held the traitor Kryvenko, but it didn't matter. On this stretch of road, only two lanes in each direction divided by a double yellow line, there was no place for those trucks to escape them. And no law enforcement officers anywhere close.

Not that police would matter much, given that he would expect one state trooper with a single revolver.

Kaz had brought a team of killers. If they were all armed with standard Colt Officer's Model pistols, that would be sufficient to kill drivers and get the trucks stopped.

Then he could slaughter all of the traitors except for the ones Moscow wanted alive. Gradskaya and Zhidkov. And the woman might suffer some along the way.

The strike team rolled off in pursuit, headed north along the highway after crossing the mountains. This was called the Las Vegas Highway by locals, running to the resort town in Nevada, having crossed the vast desert and dried lake beds to get there. They were in the middle of nowhere, surrounded by endless bald hills and scrub. Heat, but nowhere to hide.

On the negative side of the equation, the motorcycles were

loud. Men could yell over them, but not far. And controlling throttle, brake, and clutch required both hands and a lot of concentration, so he had two men on each bike except for himself.

It wouldn't slow them as much as the trucks, but each team was functionally independent.

Still, they had trained for this. Prepared mentally and physically.

Kaz had no gunner riding behind him, so he was at the rear of the formation, while Captain Yegorov led, with Sgt. Mikhaylov riding as his shooter.

Kaz watched and stayed close as Yegorov began to accelerate. Not charging, but closing to the point that they could begin their attack. Pistols came out from beneath black leather jackets.

Soon, he could go home to Moscow.

CHAPTER 26

"Color?" Vanya replied to Yuri at the head of the convoy. "The color is trouble. I see guns coming out. Alert everyone that we are being attacked."

He put the radio down with care rather than dropping it, turning to Arkadi and nodding as the man surged to his feet.

Arkadi Nenashev was the team sniper. Winchester Model 70 bolt-action sporting rifle in .30-06 Springfield. A deadly American weapon, but there were far more motorcycles rushing up behind them than Arkadi likely had bullets.

The truck had a green canvas awning stretched over the top and tied down. Sufficient for sun and wind. Presumably for rain as well, though Vanya assumed that they would still be as cold as the ones he remembered from Leningrad in the winter.

Rather than draw his pistol, Vanya knelt next to Arkadi and brought his Thompson around front, automatically locating his magazine bag and retrieving the first stick. The truck was filled with various wooden crates that held supplies, both personal and industrial. It would make a reasonable amount of cover, and Vanya had specifically chosen to ride in the bed with Arkadi, putting the spare Shore Patrol Marine up front with the driver.

Wise move, it turned out, but that had been merely Vanya's decision to spend the drive with his combat partner, rather than a complete stranger. The relationship between pilot and radar operator paled next to that of sniper and spotter.

Today, that might matter.

"Do I engage?" Arkadi asked formally, even as he chambered a round and knelt behind a box.

Someone opened fire from one of the motorcycles, rendering the question moot as they both ducked.

"They are going for the driver," Vanya called as the attackers began to accelerate.

"No," Arkadi replied. "They are not."

Vanya curbed his question as Arkadi suddenly rose to a crouch, leaned, and rotated, before firing a single shot. He dropped and racked the bolt.

On the road, one of the lead motorcycles was suddenly on fire, like an aircraft that had sustained a hit to a gas tank that wasn't self-sealing. The gang of pursuers suddenly had to maneuver and fall back, lest they all crash, which would be hideous and terminal at these speeds.

Would have helped Vanya's issues, though.

He rose, flipping the safety on his Thompson as he moved to the front of the bed and pulled at the canvas, leaning out into the wind on the passenger side.

"We are being attacked!" he yelled as he thumped the side of the cab, meeting the surprised eyes of the man in the passenger seat. "Prepare to repel boarders."

It was a navy thing, but he had heard it used by soldiers are well, in that moment when the Nazis had begun a charge with bayonets, SMGs, and grenades.

A grenade would have been nice today, but he would make do.

Vanya moved back to where Arkadi was trying to line up on madly-evading hornets so he could take another shot.

Vanya wasn't trying for precision. He leaned into his Thompson, checked that there were hardly any other cars on the road, and triggered a burst.

CHAPTER 27

Sasha was in truck number three with the window down, when Ilya thumped on the side of the cab.

"Trouble rear, Commander," his team sergeant called even as gunfire roared everywhere. "Someone going after Red-2."

Sasha looked over at the driver, a young man he didn't know, in a pretty uniform with a pistol and a truncheon.

"Be prepared to shoot back," Sasha ordered.

Ahead, Yuri's truck had already shifted lanes to the right and slowed down, one big bear arm waving Gennadi's truck to come even.

"Form a laager with truck four," Sasha said. "Leave enough space for men and women in the other trucks to shoot, but keep everyone together."

"Where are you going, sir?" the marine asked.

"To stop them," Sasha replied.

He didn't have his Thompson, but Ilya was armed. And Gennadi had needed something.

Prophetically, it seemed.

He opened the door against the wind and climbed out onto the step, catching Ilya's hand and letting the man pull him up into the bed of the truck, where a surprised American marine watched the whole performance.

Aft, he could see now where Vanya's truck was straddling two lanes, with Lyuba's still in line.

Tomorrow, he would make sure to acquire radios for everyone, but that was tomorrow's problem. Today, he had other issues.

Sasha pointed at *Banshee*'s driver and motioned that man to shift closer to the side of the road. That would create space for Vanya's truck to come up. Perhaps they needed to run four or five abreast, as he could see many motorcycles back there, all of them seemingly with two riders, one armed and one driving.

So, an assassination attempt. The other shoe falling, as it were, having failed in Dublin.

Or they had wanted to kill him and Gennadi that day and had been planning to get everyone else here.

Sasha drew his Shanxi and thumbed the safety off as he joined Ilya at the rear, slightly protected by crates, but with nothing except cloth on the sides, were one of the shooters to come even with them.

"Drive them off," Sasha yelled over the wind to the two men with him. "Assume assassins come for your soul and shoot to kill."

A rude order. Crude even, especially by his standards of conduct.

Necessary today, because they had selected a mostly abandoned stretch of road in the middle of the desert, with machines far faster than his trucks.

It would be lumbering bombers beset on all sides by Nazi Messerschmidts, all over again.

"Explosives?" Ilya called back.

"No," Sasha decided. "Too much risk while we have trucks behind us. If we drop back, go ahead, but not until then."

Ilya nodded and switched to his Thompson, slipping a stick in and racking it live while the Marine had only a pistol. And Sasha had no idea if the man had space ammunition for it.

They settled and looked for a clear shot.

CHAPTER 28

Gennadi heard the gunfire and automatically loaded his weapon.

He was too old for doing some of the crazy stunts Sasha and the others were becoming famous for, but he was still not yet fifty. And the arm and leg had reacted well to the warmth of San Diego, so he had to consider that living in a cold climate might be the problem.

Mexico might not welcome a former Soviet, but there were warm places he could go.

"Sir?" the driver asked, still uncertain about where Gennadi fit in the scheme of things.

Being introduced as Red Branch Command while dressed as a civilian, when everyone else wore blue uniforms, had likely not helped.

"What is oncoming traffic like?" Gennadi asked.

"Not hardly anything, sir," the man replied.

"Turn on all your lights and cross the median line," Gennadi ordered. "You watch for cars coming at us but stay over there. I want to take our foes in a flank."

The boy's eyes bugged out a bit, but he had many rank

stripes on his sleeve. And Gennadi had sounded just like the Air Forces Colonel that he was.

The man hunkered down, fiddled with various switches, and they slid over.

Hopefully, nobody was about to slam into the front of their Deuce and a Half at high speeds.

He would deal with that later. After all, he had survived shooting down Voss, once upon a time. And being shot down.

Gennadi was right handed, but the cab of the truck had space. He turned and braced one foot down and the other knee on the seat, looking out of the open window to a swarm of angry insects besetting Vanya's truck. Not too close, though, because smoke in the distance suggested one shot down already.

"SIR!" his driver called. "Lead truck wants us to shift all the way across."

"YES!" Gennadi yelled back. "Block the road entirely. A herd of angry cattle beset by wolves. Except that we will bite."

"Aye, aye, sir!"

Gennadi ignored the man and rested his Thompson on the windowsill, waiting for a clear shot, because the weapon simply wasn't that accurate.

Not until someone got closer.

CHAPTER 29

Lyuba had ridden in the bed of the truck with Yanina, mostly so neither of them had to listen to propositions from foolish American soldiers. Let the two men stay up front and tell sad stories and inappropriate jokes.

She glanced up and saw Vanya's truck slowing, then swerving back and forth.

Then gunfire.

The Thompson was around and she had a magazine loaded almost by magic. Yanina grabbed a large crate and slammed it against the tailgate turned sideways, providing them a level parapet and defensive protection.

Lyuba knelt and braced, wondering if the young boys up front had heard. Or recognized. Not everyone was a war veteran these days, as Germany had been crushed more than four years ago.

Still, Lyuba studied her problem. Vanya, alone. Everyone else ahead of her, but hopefully reacting.

"You shoot, I will reload," Yanina said. "I packed two extra boxes of ammunition in my kit today."

Yes.

Lyuba braced herself and tangled a hand in the shoulder strap. The barrel would be far too hot to touch shortly.

Part of a gang on motorcycles were trying to get around Vanya's truck. She could see where they were riding tandem, with the man in back holding what looked like American Colt pistols.

The range was not great for her Thompson, but six magazines and reloads would let her get a little excessive. That might be appropriate right now.

It often was.

Lyuba sighted on the lead vehicle of the mess and ripped off half of her magazine like a homicidal woodpecker. The last few rounds would go high, but she had elevation and there were many of those men trying to do something.

Shooting at the Red Branch meant that they had already become her enemy.

An engine exploded in flames, which was a pity, because she'd been intending to kill people instead. Still, it was a useful distraction, especially as that caused the vehicle to swerve to the left, cutting off half of the following mob and forcing all of them to brake savagely if they didn't want to run into their leader and become a flaming mass of parts and bodies scattered across the roadway.

Which would have helped.

They slowed down instead. Bunched up. The distance was bad and getting worse, but she emptied the rest of the magazine into them from here anyway.

Easier to hit.

Vanya's driver almost swerved into her line of fire. Might have even gotten his mirror clipped, but she wasn't paying attention and didn't really care, as she ejected her first magazine and grabbed the next one Yanina was holding for her.

She slammed it home and locked the bolt.

More trouble would come. Lyuba would be ready.

CHAPTER 30

Gennadi watched as Yuri's truck followed them across the highway, holding the entire width now.

"Driver, shift over and drop back until you are even with that truck," he ordered sharply. "Stay with them and do not let anyone pass from behind. If you have to, crush them between the bigger vehicles."

The poor man gulped, eyes huge, but he understood the heavy command authority in Gennadi's voice and nodded.

Brutal. Cruel but necessary, just as Gennadi had been correct that today might be a risk, and Sasha had brought all the firepower.

Well, not all of it. If this sort of thing was going to happen routinely, perhaps the Red Branch needed heavier weapons. A weapons team, either a heavy machine gun or maybe mortars. Or the American bazooka.

Something excessive right now might be appropriate.

Pity that they didn't have any easy way to ask those jets that had escorted Sasha to San Diego to slip down and conduct a strafing run this afternoon.

Tomorrow's problems.

He used the frame of the door as a brace, and flipped the select switch to single fire. Less risk of hitting anyone friendly as the situation devolved into a chaotic mob scene, though he was not surprised when Lyuba cut loose full auto. It had to be *Banshee* shooting from that truck, because Yanina tended to be quieter and more precise.

Gennadi fired individual shots, cursing that an American highway that had felt so much smoother than Russian roads just five minutes ago was suddenly too bumpy to be all that accurate.

Still, he had sixty rounds if he was careful. And could always get the Colt from the driver if he had to.

At least the fools on motorcycles had discovered that they had grabbed an angry tiger by the tail, as they also began to swerve madly.

Then the truck swerved, throwing him hard against the jam and cracking his skull.

"Sorry, sir," the driver said. "Oncoming wasn't paying any attention and almost plowed into us."

Gennadi rubbed what would be a goose egg later, but didn't complain. He had demanded that the driver do something dangerously foolish in the heat of battle, so he had to live with the consequences.

Gennadi braced himself harder against the frame and continued to fire individual shots.

CHAPTER 31

Sasha watched as Vanya and Lyuba's trucks moved into a line.

"Forward vehicles also lining up," Ilya said, looking out the side of the bed. "We don't block the road, but we do present an obstacle to pursuit."

He was back to bomber training. Keep everyone close and tight, where gun turrets could provide overlapping fire against German planes making runs in and through. By the time Sasha was escorting those missions, the Nazis had been largely shattered in the air, needing only the final hammer blows from Guards Heavy Armor units to finish them off.

He turned to the Marine with them. Sized up the fellow. Bantam cock. Short and feisty, but a complete stranger. Still, the young man had a pistol in one hand, hammer back and safety holding it.

Intense and intent.

"You move to the front with our driver," Sasha ordered, then overrode the smaller man's aggression. "He needs someone protecting him while we drive, because at some point, one of those motorcycles will take advantage of their greater speed to swoop by, shooting. You will kill him when he does."

The vocabulary choice was specific and intentional. This was not a day to wound someone. Not if they were conducting armed piracy on an American highway in broad daylight.

The Marine paused, nodded, and holstered his pistol.

"Aye aye, sir," he replied, then climbed out the side and into the cab.

Out of Sasha's way, and providing flank coverage, because all of his potential wingmen were in other trucks, doing the same.

Hopefully, it would be enough.

The motorcycles had fallen back some. Sasha could see several pillars of smoke in the distance, suggesting machines that had been killed, though he had no idea if the riders were down as well.

Looking out both sides, he realized that Yuri and Gennadi had lined all five trucks up abreast, blocking the entire width save for the ditches where an ambitious rider could get around them, because the trucks were too top-heavy at this speed. Someone would tip over if they tried.

Hopefully, the outer two drivers understood that, and were good enough to ride right to the edge, forcing his attackers to attempt it.

That, or make them give up and withdraw in the face of heavily armed Soviet troops with stable firing platforms and no particular interest in playing nice.

Sasha certainly wasn't. Lyuba, neither. In fact, at this point, Sasha doubted that any of the men and women under his command, including Gennadi today, would spare any troublemakers.

He turned to Ilya, one eye on machine still some hundred meters back.

"What explosives do you have for this kind of situation?" he asked carefully.

Ilya smiled that little smile that suggested a soldier sandbagging for inspection. Or a pop quiz.

He dug into his bag and pulled out a pair of American-made grenades that Sasha had not requisitioned. Nor known about.

As with Oleg, there were times when a smart commander developed a certain willful blindness. Especially when he had top notch troops who were pulling on the chain and needed to be restrained, rather than slackers who had to be kicked and shoved into performing.

Sasha bit his tongue and nodded. Ilya was an expert with such things. That and his rank as team sergeant had gotten him a place with the Red Branch.

"On their next attack run, you will use one," Sasha yelled over the wind. "Save the other for now, just in case."

Ilya nodded and slipped his Thompson around back. Sasha considered taking the weapon, but decided that his Shanxi would be sufficient, especially as the rest of the team was ready to engage.

Ilya's head came up, causing Sasha to turn to look.

"Here they come."

CHAPTER 32

Yuri considered moving aft to help Oleg and Dmitri, but he needed to be serving as Red-Base right now, watching forward and maintaining radio contact with Vanya more than they needed one more gun facing aft.

He kept his eyes forward, in case the motorcycles were a trap. Hounds driving the fox to a hunter lying in wait. There were pitifully few places to hide around here, but it would only take one sniper like Arkadi to shoot out a tire and force the convoy to stop to protect them.

A herd of angry cattle protecting calves from the wounded.

"Make sure you keep watch for an ambush ahead," Yuri yelled to his driver. "As well as oncoming traffic that we will let pass between us on our left."

"Should we open a space now, sir?" the man countered.

Yuri considered it.

"Yes," he said. "One car width, so drivers have a corridor. And it might entice our foolish friends into attempting it the other direction."

Rather than reply, the Shore Patrolman drew his pistol and rested it in his lap where he could get to it quickly.

Yuri saw Gennadi's look of surprise across the way, so he tried to signal to Red Branch Command that this was on purpose. And a trap. The wind would swallow any words.

"Vanya, this is Yuri," he said into the radio. "We are opening a path on the left of the formation, into oncoming traffic, to allow cars going the other way to pass safely. I assume trouble will see that and attack."

"Understood," Vanya called back after a moment. "We'll keep watch here."

Yuri nodded and watched forward, certain that nothing would come up behind them without being met.

What was in front of them?

CHAPTER 33

Vanya put the radio back down and considered the tactical situation. Sasha and Lyuba were the fiery, emotional ones. Gennadi had been a pilot, but Vanya hadn't seen the man in battle to know what he would be like. Yuri was operating as Red-Base, off to one side and protecting the entire force from surprises.

That left him and Arkadi as the calm, logical ones, but that was exactly what you wanted in a sniper team.

"Can you identify leaders?" he asked Arkadi.

"One bike at the very rear only has a single rider," Arkadi replied immediately. "That first machine I killed, at the beginning, was leading the others, so it might have been a team sergeant, or even a junior officer, if we presume a senior like Sasha on the solo. The others react well like a trained team of insertion troopers. The kind that travel behind enemy lines to disrupt or assassinate."

"Will your rifle kill two men, if you get a square hit?" Vanya pressed.

"It should," Arkadi nodded. ".30-06 is a heavy cartridge,

firing copper-jacketed rounds intended to penetrate at a reasonable distance."

"Go ahead and shoot at them now," Vanya ordered. "I have my Thompson you can have when you run out of ammunition, so I will use my pistol after this. Better we knock them down now."

"Why would they attack like this?" Arkadi asked.

"Someone expected pilots and flight crew, Arkadi," Vanya replied as his sniper began to settle in to shoot. "They were not prepared for us to be armed as a ground commando. Nor to be willing to engage them with lethal force instantly. It is a mistake that they will not make a second time, but that presumes we give them such a chance."

"Third time, sir," Arkadi said as he fired a shot with a snapping crack. "Dublin was first."

Vanya watched one of those enemy machines suddenly drive off the side of the road, hitting the softer gravel and dirt and tumbling forward, two riders ejected into the sands.

He would presume they were either already dead, or about to be.

And as if that was the signal, the rest suddenly charged.

CHAPTER 34

Lyuba had enough ammunition to get crazy, plus her pistol with two spare magazines as well, though the shorter barrel meant that she needed to wait until they were much closer for that.

The Thompson was a lovely weapon at fifty meters, but at two or three times that, accuracy was sorely lacking. She wondered if anyone was making some sort of battle rifle that was capable of full-auto or select fire, using a better cartridge, capable of deadly accuracy at two hundred meters. The Nazis had had their StG 44, but nobody else had yet emulated them.

She had to wait for them to get close, at high closure speed, and then pick them off. Others were using single shots, but Lyuba understood that to be merely pinpricks.

Shortly, they would be unleashing hell.

Now, as a matter of fact. Even over the sound of the wind and road, she heard all the engines back there rev loudly, belching smoke as the enemy charged.

Yanina nodded and continued loading the last empty stick magazine from the box between her thighs, four full ones ready to go, in addition to the fifth in Lyuba's weapon.

She considered how the enemy would attack. They seemed to be leaning to the right, beyond Sasha's truck where she would not get a clear shot at them once they got close, so Lyuba noted her next reload and began firing full-auto even at this range. She might get lucky. She might distract.

More importantly, it would give her time to drop an empty magazine and slam a fresh one home to continue firing when the enemy got to an optimum range for her to enfilade them.

Nose-on, they were a small target. That would change as they closed, geometry working in her favor.

She fired off the entire stick in one hideous roar then reached for the next.

CHAPTER 35

Kaz had been deeply surprised when the trucks had been so heavily armed. Captain Yegorov had lost his machine at the very beginning of the battle, but they had already been moving past so quickly that Kaz hadn't had a chance to determine if the rider had been killed with his mount.

Around him, Kaz felt the team wavering, caught midway between rage at having already taken casualties for no gain and concern that they might have bitten off more than they could chew in attacking this convoy.

The Traitor was a pilot. All of his team were fliers of some sort. How had they gotten so good at small unit tactics? And to be so heavily armed?

Next time, Kaz would bring something matching them for firepower. He doubted that he could steal American warplanes, or find something capable of an aerial duel, but the Traitor wasn't aloft all the time. He could be ambushed on the ground, though Kaz understood that he would need to bring utterly overwhelming force with him next time. Perhaps a full assault battalion of troops, instead of a scout platoon with pistols.

His mistake in underestimating them.

Around him, the surviving bikers—surviving? How many had he lost already?—were looking to him, with Yegorov gone.

Ahead, a gap had opened between the first and second truck on his left, no doubt to allow oncoming vehicles to pass if they were smart and quick to react.

It felt like a trap, but the only other option at this point seemed to be walking away and returning to pick up anyone he could find still alive.

"Follow me!" he yelled as loud as he could, then opened the throttle with an even louder roar and charged.

Ahead and to his right, he saw a driver and rider both slump at the same time. Saw the vehicle fall out of line and drift, understanding that someone had killed the two even at this range.

He had to do this now, or run. Simple as that.

General Chaykovsky would not be interested in excuses, because his orders had been fairly clear that Kaz would come home with his shield or on it.

Time to find out which.

CHAPTER 36

Gennadi saw them coming. Saw the enemy unit waver, then the solo rider machine waved a hand and charged, like that first ME109 coming out of the sun.

Banshee wailed at them fully automatic, as expected. Others also began firing, but the roads were bumpy and the targets weaving madly to evade.

He hoped that Yuri's driver would understand what was coming.

At least once it was upon them.

Gennadi turned to his driver and waved a hand, then pointed back.

"They are coming," he said loud enough to be heard. "Let them. When they are in the killing zone, I want you to swerve into the truck on this side and crush them. Our vehicles will absorb far more damage than theirs will, and we can always pull over and await help if either of these trucks suffer sufficient damage. We are also close enough to Muroc that they might be watching and trying to figure out what to do."

"Really, sir?" the man asked. "Run them over?"

"Like bugs," Gennadi ordered. "I want you paying attention, so that you do not lose control of the truck when it happens. We can always fix a flat tire, but I'd rather not the truck tumble ass over tea kettle. Am I clear?"

Hard voice. He understood that.

Red Branch Command. And before that, a Colonel in the GRU. The military wing of the Main Intelligence Directorate. The *Главное разведывательное управление* itself.

It required hard men and women. Hard enough to accept orders to defect to the West and live and perhaps die as an outlaw, because that was the only way to hunt down those treacherous bastards that should have been executed at Nuremberg. And there were thousands that the Americans had let get away, in addition to some that should have never been allowed to survive, even serving the American government.

Likely, he could never go home. Would have to live a lie for the rest of his days. But if it involved helping Sasha save the world from the forces of chaos and evil, even in Soviet uniforms, that was a price worth paying, because nobody could possibly win an atomic war.

Not when Comrade Stalin had the bomb as well.

That was the price too high to pay.

The Marine gulped and nodded, both hands on the steering wheel and shoulders braced.

"I will watch, then drop into the footwell so I am not bouncing around," he called, putting his weapon on safety and stowing it.

The last thing he needed was an accidental discharge now, when he might hit his driver. Or Nikon and the other Marine who were riding in the bed and presumably defending them like proper tailgunners.

"Here they come."

CHAPTER 37

Nikon knew close combat. The Chinese Open Hand forms that he had learned from that one ancient Comrade with skin like leather and the softest touch of any human he had ever encountered.

And he knew melee weapons. *Jian. Dao. Rochin. Quandao.* Sticks of various lengths and lethality, from a simple cane up to a Monk's Spade.

Today, he was holding his Thompson. Not his best weapon, but he didn't offer to trade the American soldier for that one's pistol.

Nikon had noted the gap between vehicles, closed initially, then opened more recently. He understood that Red Branch Command had baited a trap.

In close combat, you intentionally left certain openings in your defenses. A lesser opponent might see it and think it a mistake they could exploit, flowing into a counter already in place and leaving themselves doomed.

The wise opponent would ignore it and do their own thing instead, forcing you to dance to their tune if both fighters were intent on combat.

Sometimes, after several seconds, both would realize that they were closely matched experts, where a battle might require hours or even days according to some legends, in order to come to a draw anyway.

In some stories, those great masters stepped back, bowed to one another, and got roaring drunk as blood brothers, five minutes after meeting.

This Marine Shore Patrol soldier was not about to become a member of the Red Branch, so Nikon flipped his weapon to full automatic and squared his shoulders, bracing his feet in a proper stance to absorb all the recoil he was about to unleash.

Pa Qua. Walking the circle. Understanding that he would be shooting into a narrow range, where his natural exuberance might cause him to rotate inward and shoot at Oleg and Dmitri in the next truck over.

Unacceptable. At the same time, he understood that putting every bullet he had downrange at the appropriate moment would be called for. If someone was stupid enough to try to climb into the bed with them, he would use his Thompson like a club.

Whoever had designed the weapon had expected that, and made it heavy enough for such a thing.

The soldier was taking aimed shots. Not hitting anything, but that weapon was for short range and calm conditions.

Exactly what they did not have today.

Today, his job was to bring chaos.

The legendary Irish Hunt that saw his officers earn their nicknames.

He would be their hound.

Motorcycles closed at high speed. Others immediately opened fire, but Nikon understood that they would have several seconds reloading, exactly at the moment when his foes were close enough for their own pistols to become accurate.

He would wait.

Then he would pounce.

CHAPTER 38

Sasha saw them coming. Like Nazi fighters in a swooping line, throttles open as they exploded into motion. What they thought they could do against a line of heavy trucks eluded him, but he also understood that he had limited situational awareness.

His own universe was a pie-slice of visibility aft, filled with the roar of guns and engines, even as he held his fire for now. With that many machine guns speaking, his Shanxi wasn't going to tip the balance, but he might see something critical if he paid attention.

One leader, riding solo. A dozen and more other bikes, all with a second rider. The armed ones preparing to fire as they got close.

For once, he was glad that the 1911 Colt .45 was so common in the US. A powerful slug, but only at short range and not all that accurate from such a weapon. Firing into the heavy wind as you rode would slow them down even more, to the point that those bikers would have to be almost on top of the trucks to have any accuracy.

And he doubted that they had brought the sorts of

combat-necessary reloads that he had ordered his team to bring today.

Not that he had expected this, but Dublin had left him subconsciously expecting something.

He hoped that it would be enough.

They charged.

Sasha understood that the heavy trucks were probably traveling at more than eighty kilometers per hour, but those bikes were an engine with wheels, and likely capable of double that, even with two riders.

The rate of closure was stunning, but they had to come right at him, it felt, and all of his team seemed to have expected this, because the sound of machine guns was suddenly overwhelming, like that Hebrew Joshua and his trumpet.

Or Stalin's Organs firing their Katyusha rockets into the night.

Sasha had knelt behind a crate and braced. He began firing carefully. Not aiming at a point but at a line where he expected the bikers to intersect, like how American fighter aircraft during the war had frequently parallaxed their wing guns at a certain range.

Nose cannons gave you better control, but he was off-line.

"Give them the other one now," Sasha yelled at Ilya. "This is the battle."

Ilya tossed a pin out the back, followed a moment later by the grenade, hurled with some force so that it hit, tumbled, and rolled after the trucks, but at a distance.

He ignored the man after that, other than to note a third grenade following the secone. Either that first toss had gone wrong, or the enemy had understood, because they had swerved away from the explosion. The second one herded them even more to his right, but caught at least one that suddenly fell out of line, then fell over and began to skid before hitting something and jumping in the air shedding parts.

Or bodies.

Sasha found that he was beyond caring, either way. They had attacked him. And pushed the attack instead of backing off when confronted by someone that could fight back against a bully.

That was a thing he understood as well.

Bullies usually only understand greater force. They live to hurt people weaker than them, and only withdraw when confronted by superior force.

He had brought all the guns today. And the killers to use them.

More bikes went down as the Red Branch spoke. Not all of them, but the survivors were going to be paying a terrible toll for this.

Maybe he'd get all of them.

CHAPTER 39

Gennadi watched and counted. Heard the tremendous racket as the Red Branch opened up. And someone, presumably Ilya Markov, had brought grenades.

Not enough of them, and the situation did not lend itself well to such a thing, but Gennadi was hard-pressed to think what might work better, save for a shaped charge across the rear bumper of the truck, filled with ball bearings that could be detonated into the enemy ranks as they got too close.

He made a mental note to ask Markov later. Presumably, that one had either built or thought about building such a device at some point.

There had been a reason Gennadi had selected him over some of the other candidates.

The enemy column closed, engines roaring louder than before, so Gennadi presumed they intended to shoot this gap and get ahead of the convoy where they could bottle his force up entirely.

"STAND BY!" Gennadi yelled, understanding that he was in his driver's way to see the mirror on this side, but he needed to time this just right.

Especially at these speeds.

Gennadi counted down in his head, watching tailgunners make themselves felt, but not enough of them were hitting.

As with bombers and interceptors, there was too much randomness, even at this range, to score easy kills.

He would need turret-mounted weapons for that sort of accuracy. Which, in turn, suggested an armored scout car like the British had generally perfected during the war.

Idly, he wondered if the Americans would sell him a transport aircraft large enough to carry such a thing. And if he could convince Sasha to paint it blue.

The lead vehicle was almost there. Gennadi watched the lone rider thread the needle. He could have ordered the crush now, but that would give the others behind him a chance to brake and perhaps evade their destruction.

Gennadi wanted more of them dead.

He nodded. Slipped into the footwell and braced himself as best he could with good arm and leg. The bad ones were behaving, but he didn't dare push them. Not today.

"NOW!" he yelled as loud as he could, then squeezed every which way as the truck turned into a horse attempting to buck off its rider.

The world ended.

It was even worse than slamming into the ground when his La-7 had been shot down, skimming across rough terrain and apparently chopping one wing off on a tree he'd never seen, then coming to rest in a burning aircraft, only alive because a Guards Tank unit had been close enough to pull him from the wreckage and get him to a field hospital in time.

Gennadi understood that his driver had taken the orders to heart when he felt the mass of this truck bump into Yuri's, up some because there was at least one motorcycle under the rear axle.

Fire had slacked off, though he wasn't sure how he knew that, save that a moment later it redoubled in intensity.

No doubt, the surviving bikers caught at slow speed as they braked, right in the killzone for all the Thompson submachine guns Sasha had brought today.

"Sir, are you okay?" Gennadi heard over the racket.

It took him a moment to understand. His driver, yelling.

He turned and nodded to the man. The road was smooth now, but the truck had a thump to it. Possibly a broken axle, but this felt more like a tire knocked out of alignment.

If it was his truck, he might care, but it was merely a tool, and Gennadi had already decided to use them all up today, if that was what it took to survive.

To win.

It was painful, climbing out and up. His goose egg was prominent when he touched it, but he didn't feel a concussion coming on. Merely pain, which was an old enemy he would overcome like he always did.

Instead of looking, he turned and sat. Saw one bike, ahead in the distance and pulling away at fantastic speeds.

It was probably too much to ask that the man suffer a mechanical breakdown after all this.

"What happened?" he yelled, breathing.

"Got three of them, I think," the Marine yelled back. "One more bounced off my bumper. The rest slowed down. Your people annihilated them when they did. That guy's going away like a roadrunner."

"Can we make it to Muroc?" Gennadi asked.

He glanced over and saw Yuri's driver. Beside them, but not that close. He waved at both.

Yuri was indicating that they should pull over, so perhaps one of trucks was too wounded to continue, though Gennadi understood that there were times when you had to give it everything you had.

Sometimes, you even survived.

"We could, but I think they want to stop," his driver replied. "What are your orders, sir?"

Red Branch Command. Only Sasha could pull rank on him, and then, Sasha only would if he thought the situation warranted it.

"Are there any more motorcycles?" he asked the man.

"Not in one piece, no," came the reply. "Lots of dead people scattered on the highway, but I'm not sure I want to go back and find out if they're playing possum."

Gennadi agreed with that. It would only take one lunatic with his own grenades to ruin everything.

Still, the situation was unknown. And there were four other trucks that had been involved as well.

"Find a safe spot to pull over," Gennadi ordered the man. "Let us see where we stand."

CHAPTER 40

Sasha walked up to Gennadi's truck, marveling at the damage and even more impressed that it seemed to be driveable. He hadn't seen what had happened, save that most of the attackers had suddenly stopped short. Where the Red Branch had been waiting with machine guns.

Dmitri and Ilya were inspecting the vehicle with two of the marines, so he gathered his officers together and split the enlisted into two teams, watching both ends for any other trouble that might arrive.

"What happened?" he asked Gennadi as they stood off to one side.

"I ordered my driver to leave a gap for the attackers," Gennadi replied calmly, Thompson in hand and pointed up. Immediately ready at hand. "He did. Yuri's driver did the same. They attempted to run the gauntlet. I ordered him to swerve in and crush them before they could escape me."

Sasha blinked, mostly at the calm way Gennadi described such an action.

Utterly emotionless, worse than even Vanya on many days.

"One did get away," Gennadi continued, gesturing everyone

close, even as he looked around. "And that one presents a most troubling, but in retrospect probably expected, problem."

"Why is that?" Sasha asked, noting that Yuri, Lyuba, and Vanya all looked over other shoulders to keep a clear perimeter.

Such were Gennadi's tones affecting them.

"Because I recognized the man," Gennadi said simply.

"You recognized him, Gennadi?" Vanya asked sharply. "From where?"

"Moscow," Gennadi said bluntly. "Last time I encountered him, he was a colonel in the Main Intelligence Directorate. The GRU itself."

"Are you suggesting that the men we killed today are a Soviet attack commando?" Sasha asked.

"*Spetsialnogo Naznacheniya*," Gennadi replied, lowering his voice. "*Spetsnatz* for short. Special Operations troops, usually trained to infiltrate deep behind enemy lines. Disruption. Assassination. Interdiction. Whatever is necessary and appropriate for Soviet forces."

"That suggests that Moscow is trying to kill us," Lyuba offered darkly. "Do they not understand the mission that they gave us?"

"On the contrary, it means that our cover has not been pierced, even in Moscow," Sasha replied. "Remember, we were originally sent to hunt war criminals. And have been successful there. Stopping the Werewolf Legion, however, has irretrievably raised our profile, to the point that the Americans have offered to house and fund us."

"What happens if they ever discover the truth?" Yuri asked.

"They will possibly arrest us as spies," Vanya interjected. "But remember, they have hired us to also hunt those same people, though perhaps they would want to shelter certain criminals that Moscow might want dead. Does anything change about our overall mission?"

Sasha turned to Gennadi. Red Branch Command, though Sasha was the field leader.

GRU Colonel Gennadi Nazarenko had created this tool.

And now, apparently, the same GRU was trying to kill them.

"Sasha is correct," Gennadi said. "Our cover is intact. And we might be at war with our own forces, but I selected all of you understanding that such a thing might happen. Do not tell me now, but if you find that to be too much to accept, let me know quietly and we will find a way to get you home. I remain Red Branch Command."

Sasha looked at the other three and got nods.

They had known going in, but perhaps not to this level of certainty. And they had just wiped cut a hit team sent to kill them all. In California. Not all that far from Muroc Field that would be Edwards Air Force Base soon.

"We must get to safety," Sasha announced. "If this truck cannot make it, we abandon it and load everything into one of the others. I am not aware of any injuries save yours, Gennadi, so we can get to Muroc in another few hours at most. Then we will update Lockwood and whichever generals or admirals need to get involved.

"Marines have generals," Gennadi said absently. "Only the US Navy uses admirals."

"Good enough," Sasha said. "Our secret is safe. Our mission remains. No Nazis will be allowed to escape us, save the ones that the Americans have put beyond our reach. We will get home safe and take stock. I am certain that someone has contacted the police by now, but with any luck we can outrun that news to Muroc and let Washington keep the secret instead."

"What do we tell Mr. Walker?" Lyuba asked, eyes glittering. "He is coming to interview us again, at Lockwood's invitation."

"Ask me again tomorrow," Sasha nodded. "It won't be the whole truth, but it will be enough about this to make yet more enemies."

"And allies," Vanya noted with a dry smile. "We have just destroyed a dangerous criminal gang, intent on hijacking cargo trucks crossing the desert. We can play up that element of things and let the average American come to associate the Red Branch with law and order and safety, because we have really begun down that road as well, when you look at it thus."

"You think of a way to explain it and let me know," Sasha ordered, confident that a former commissar like Vanya would know exactly what phrases to use, because this was as much truth and news as propaganda.

If you could drive even a single sheet of paper between the two.

CHAPTER 41

Gennadi was still somewhat surprised that his truck made it, but his driver had simply stated that he would make it happen. And then had done so.

Guards at the gate were far more heavily armed than usual, from what he understood from the others. Thompsons like his, instead of merely pistols. And nearly a dozen such men, instead of only a pair.

Someone had heard the news, it seemed. Found the rubble strewn across the highway, perhaps.

And the bodies.

Idly, he wondered if he was facing civilian arrest, on top of everything else, this entire affair being far more in the shadows than one might have understood.

Until a few hours ago.

They followed Yuri's truck to a corner of the base well away from the other hangars, which he approved of. Keep the outsiders at a safe distance, especially if they brought excessive violence with them.

Into a hangar, sunlight turning suddenly to gloom before his eyes began to adapt. Heat to cool.

More soldiers. Airmen, he thought the Americans called them. Armed. Heavily, like those at the gates. Concerned, rather than aggressive.

"Thank you for managing," Gennadi said to his driver as the man pulled into line beside Yuri.

"Wouldn't have missed it, sir," the man replied brightly. "Only sorry I didn't get to shoot."

"You killed more of them than I did," Gennadi said starkly. "More of them than likely at least half of the team. Keep that in mind."

Gennadi didn't wait for a response, instead climbing down and working to ignore the stains on the side of his vehicle. Dirt and dust, adhering to sticky substances.

Like blood.

He slung the Thompson on his back and noted a cluster of Air Force blue officers nearby. Gennadi headed that way, noting that Brigadier General Lockwood Carlyle was among them.

And was outranked by a man with three stars on each shoulder. Lieutenant General. Subordinate to only a full General or Marshal of the Soviet Union. Or whatever the US Air Force called Arnold these days.

Sasha was approaching the man. Gennadi forced his legs to carry him with equal speed and stability, even as much as they hurt.

"I got a call from the highway patrol about thirty minutes ago," Lockwood began as they stepped close, ignoring social niceties. Or introducing the senior officer present. "Something about an army truck convoy being attacked in the desert. And leaving a mess on the highway."

"It was necessary to use excessive brutality as a paintbrush today, General," Gennadi spoke first. "They attacked us. We defended ourselves. Sasha had brought superior firepower. I may have broken one of your trucks when I ordered my driver to run over some of the motorcycles attempting to hijack the convoy."

He was replying to Lockwood, but ignored him and addressed the other General instead. Drawing a line in the sand, as it were.

The man recoiled a touch. Paled a shade. Whether at the tone or the content was irrelevant.

Not a man used to getting his hands dirty. Few flying officers were.

Air combat tended to be a clean affair. Right until the point your Lavochkin La-7 was on fire and you were fighting for your life to come in flat instead of nose-down. That he had succeeded was testified by being here today, though Gennadi didn't remember much after impact.

Still, ground forces understood dirt and muck.

"You folks ready to be debriefed?" Lockwood asked in a much more polite and friendly tone than he had begun with. "Everybody seems to be walking. Gennadi, do you need a doc?"

He touched the goose egg on his skull carefully, but it seemed fine. And he'd had concussions in his life that had been far worse than this. It would largely vanish in a day or two, save for a black eye as the blood and fluid drained inside.

"I need coffee," Gennadi said simply. "Then a talk that should be held behind closed doors and under an extremely high security rating."

Again, the glance at the stranger with three stars. A hint suggesting that the man might not be cleared for such information, in spite of his rank.

Back home, many things were intentionally compartmentalized thus. Nobody knew about the origins of the Red

Branch save General Shuysky, it seemed, which was for the best.

The general nodded. Shallow. Almost invisible, but present.

"What about the enlisted?" the stranger asked.

"We'll need them if you want the full story," Gennadi replied. "Your drivers, not as much, as most of those people were with Red Branch personnel at the key moments, so you might interview them separately later."

As in, those men should not know the truth. If anything, when snippets of the story got out, they would likely blow it out of proportion to make themselves look good. Perhaps fighting off an entire armored battalion, or something equally ludicrous.

Gennadi lived in a world where carefully using fragments of the truth was even more effective than outright fabrications, much of the time.

"Guns?" Lockwood asked.

"I intend to remain armed, General Carlyle," Gennadi told him. "I suspect that the others feel the same way."

"I was afraid you were gonna say that," Lockwood replied.

Gennadi shared a smile with Sasha and they fell into the stranger's wake.

CHAPTER 42

Lockwood studied the entire Red Branch.

He'd met all of them previously. Gotten to know the officers pretty damned well before this, especially Sasha and Lyuba. Gennadi Nazarenko was a bit of a cipher, but spoke with the calm assurance of a senior officer, though Lockwood had never gotten the whole truth out of the man.

Lt. General Stoddard, Lockwood's boss in many ways, had moved off to one side, largely to listen today, without contributing anything, so Lockwood had moved to the head of the table and asked Sasha for a breakdown. Vanya had spoken instead, walking them down from the top when he'd seen a motorcycle gang suddenly race up from behind and draw pistols.

At that point, it had gotten ugly, but he'd already sent some mechanics out and gotten reports of fresh bullet holes in the sides and rear of the trucks, as well as the wood crates holding gear.

"Another Hollister Riot?" Stoddard asked at one point.

"I am unfamiliar with the term, sir," Sasha replied politely.

Stoddard grimaced, possibly regretting talking, but Lockwood had no idea what the man was referring to, either.

Turned out to be a small riot by a bunch of hooligans on motorcycles back in '47, up the coast closer to San Francisco, but Lockwood knew that Los Angeles had a few similar subcultures of criminal activity. Some left over from running rum and drugs up from Mexico during Prohibition. Some just because it was nicer here year-around, when riding a motorcycle in the snow and rain had to suck.

"Should the military or the FBI investigate this one, sir?" Lockwood asked when Stoddard stopped speaking. He got a nod. "I'll send a note to both to send resources. Gennadi, you mentioned a few things that required Top Secret?"

He liked the way that *everyone* in here turned to Lt. General Stoddard at the same time. Made Lockwood feel a lot better than they accepted him and saw his boss as the outsider. Especially after hearing what they'd just done on an American highway.

Lockwood could only imagine what the newspapers would be like when they got hold of this. Good thing he had Addison Walker coming out on a train to interview everyone as part of the Dublin attack.

Except that two such attacks in short order suggested a deeper problem.

Yeah, he could see Sasha and Gennadi being tight-lipped.

"I have the highest security clearance of anyone in this room," Stoddard announced in a frosty voice.

Lockwood decided to play nice for now. Whatever it was, it was likely to come out anyway. Better if it did as part of somebody's enemies getting ugly. After all, Sasha had immediately understood that Stalin detonating an a-bomb might change everything they'd previously agreed on.

How much worse could it get?

Except that Gennadi had a look in his eyes that made Lockwood regret even asking that in the confines of his own head.

"Who do you work for?" Gennadi asked simply, apparently willing to play hardball with Stoddard, which normally would be fun to watch.

Maybe less to today.

"The Joint Chiefs of Staff in DC," Stoddard replied. "That's all you need to know."

Lockwood knew more, but he was also Stoddard's direct liaison from Defense Intelligence to the CIA and a few others. And Sasha didn't need to know that. Nor did Gennadi.

Gennadi nodded. Smiled. Turned to look at the others and include them in his smile. Lockwood wondered what level of bullshit the man was about to unleash. It had that feel to it, and nobody had been able to penetrate Gennadi's history to date.

"I flew during the war," Gennadi told Stoddard, turning back to the man. "Injured in the last weeks of fighting over Berlin, and then six months in a hospital and in rehabilitation."

He waited for Stoddard to nod before proceeding.

"In 1946, I stumbled onto an interesting secret that the Soviet Marshals and leaders had hidden from everyone else," Gennadi said. "The Nazis had looted the gold of every nation they had invaded, both the national stocks as well as any individual holdings, which were rendered illegal to own. Most of it got shipped to Berlin, where a great deal of it was melted down, recast with new numbers, and sold off in places like Switzerland and Sweden."

Again the pause. Lockwood knew about those sort of things. Uncle Sam had leaned hard on both countries in '45 to clean up their acts or be lumped in with the Nazis when this was done, which would have been an ugly fate for their studied neutrality.

"I worked for Soviet Military Intelligence, but not in the field," Gennadi said calmly.

It still hit Lockwood like a punch in the stomach. Stoddard didn't seem to be doing any better.

A commie spy? Here in Muroc? Shit.

"One of the reports I came across was that the Germans had attempted to smuggle all of their remaining gold out at the end," Gennadi offered. "Sometimes they failed, as with those various mines and cave systems in Bavaria that Eisenhower and Patton found that summer. Sometimes, they almost succeeded. Gold is heavy. A ton of the metal is a cube forty centimeters on a side. Sixteen inches for an American. Hard to ship. Requires a lot of effort and tends to be visible, because trucks appear empty, even as they sag on their axles with the mass. And with the Red Army closing in, sometimes all those people could do was bury it and hope to come back later."

His smile had grown fierce. That was the word the occurred to Lockwood as he listened.

"Sometimes, high-ranking Soviet officers captured those men, and got the locations of such hordes, but decided to leave the metal in place rather than digging it up and turning it in," Gennadi continued. "Not everyone was loyal to the system."

"What are you telling me, Gennadi?" Lockwood asked pointedly, feeling like the straight man in a vaudeville routine.

"That the Soviet Union had no use for a broken husk like me," Gennadi said. "A job pushing papers around, and not much more. Until perhaps I came across such an interesting paper. And knew that Stalin was an old man with no obvious successors, so his death was going to set up another purge. Another Terror, perhaps. So I stole some of the stolen German gold. And because I was a pilot, I understood aircraft and such. I fled to the West, where a few connections were able to help me at both ends. Gold has no provenance to many people, so you can use it to do things. Here, I knew that the next purge would create a great many martyrs unnecessarily, so I used my old connections to identify people like Sasha and Yuri and spirit them out of prison cells. The others came later, because the maneuvering to replace Stalin has begun, gentlemen. And the gold has mostly vanished into the banking system and turned into money."

"How much money?" Stoddard asked quietly.

"A cube—a ton—translates almost exactly to an eighth over one million dollars," Gennadi replied. "Much more than that."

Shit, that was a lot, but a mercenary company was expensive to start and to run. Worse, when you have to buy, build, and repair jet aircraft.

At the same time, all the spies involved had corroborated Sasha and *Banshee*'s stories about the Wing and the Silver Eagle. And someone *nobody* knew was trying to kill them, both in Ireland and here in California.

Lockwood caught Stoddard's surprise, gone almost as quickly as it appeared. Might be hell to pay later. Might not. Stealing commie gold might actually earn Gennadi points with the right people.

"What were you intending with the Red Branch you created, Nazarenko?" Stoddard finally asked bluntly.

"To hunt down other Nazis," Gennadi replied. "The important ones who might have gotten away with more gold. The kind that needed to be converted to cash when the Swiss and Swedish banks suddenly closed their gold windows. That led us to the Werewolf Legion. Twice, as a matter of fact, though we merely saved the world on those occasions. But have you ever wondered how Voss and Gerstenberger were able to afford some of the things they've done? To buy those fighters or build those other aircraft?"

Okay, low blow. Lockwood was willing to admit that. And that Gennadi was right. Lockwood was used to being part of the American government, with a lot of cash and power behind him.

Nazi Germany was destroyed, a few hard-headed punks notwithstanding in their South American dreams of some silly-ass Fourth Reich. Like those Confederate yahoos in Brazil.

But a LOT of gold had vanished along the way. Even with what some of the outside players had been willing to admit, plus what the Ruskies had probably stolen and not come clean about, lest they have to give it back.

Idly, Lockwood wondered if that made him accessory, save that Sasha and *Banshee* had saved the world. Twice with Vanya and Yuri. And that Pavel guy might have been a Ruskie spy inserted in their organization to stop them, then got himself killed instead.

That fit all the details he knew.

"And the attacks?" Lockwood asked. "How do they fit in here?"

Gennadi locked eyes with Stoddard. Locked wills maybe, and was probably one of the few people stubborn enough to win. Him and Sasha, both.

"The attack in Dublin was a complete surprise," Gennadi replied. "You and Sasha helped capture the men, but I have not heard any details since then. It was today's attack that crystallized things for me."

"How so?"

"Because I recognized the one man who got away from us,"

Gennadi intoned in a sepulchral voice. "From Moscow. From the same Military Intelligence organization that I defected from, if you wanted to call it that. Fled, one step ahead of the same sorts of capital punishments that I am sure await all of us if we are ever captured and dragged back to Moscow."

"Military Intelligence?" Stoddard gasped. "Soviet?"

"The same," Gennadi said. "I have no idea what name he might be using today, but he was Colonel Kazimir Matveev when I knew him. I know his face, and presume he knows who we are, to have launched such a bold, if doomed, attack against the Red Branch. He got away. I suggest that you ask your CIA to get involved with the whoever else, because I have no doubts that those men are more than merely criminal hoodlums, though that would make a fantastic cover identity, if you wanted to insert a team behind enemy lines."

"Like the Red Branch?" Stoddard snapped.

"You invited us," Gennadi snapped back. "I was happy in Ireland. The team was making good money in South America. Once Johnson finishes his new aircraft design, I hope that we will be able to continue operating with you. If not, I would appreciate the courtesy of letting us get as far as Mexico instead of being arrested. Especially three months after you hailed us as heroes publicly."

Lockwood went ahead and jammed his teeth together rather than reply and get himself in between those two. Easy way to get crushed, with as much emotion as was on the table.

"This is unnecessary," Sasha interrupted sharply. "We are here to work. We have given immense value, I think. I would hope we can continue as before. As Gennadi has said, this is something for the highest levels of security clearance, and the General here apparently satisfies that. Our story, all of us collected that are the Red Branch, we know. I have told Lockwood about Gennadi sneaking into that prison to ask if I preferred to be executed or to be given a second chance. Everyone here faced similar circumstances. And made similar choices. Evil exists. It walks free in many places, because everyone has a different opinion of what evil is, but what the Werewolf Legion attempted fits. They are still fighting the last war. I would prefer it to be the Last War, as Wells once suggested, but until everyone comes to their senses, someone must stand up for what is right, regardless of uniform or flag."

Lockwood had warned Stoddard about Sasha, but hearing about it and feeling it were two different things.

He turned to the General and waited. Stoddard held the trump cards here, if he wanted. Air Force Intelligence at the highest level. Lockwood's eventual boss when you got close to the top of the pyramid itself.

The room fell silent, waiting.

Stoddard turned and Lockwood felt the weight of his gaze.

"Get the FBI involved directly," he ordered. "Contact CIA and have them get someone here to pick Nazarenko's brain about this Soviet spy. Ask law enforcement for information about the gang and where to find them so they can be arrested."

"Sir, if I may?" Sasha asked.

All heads rotated to *Cernunnos*.

"They've come after me and mine twice now," Sasha said. "With your permission, I'd like to return the favor."

"Bombing an American city?" Stoddard sneered.

"No," Sasha said. "As those men discovered today, the Red Branch is also trained and equipped to operate on the ground when hunting our Nazi foes. And have. We'll go after them where they live. Although, if necessary, I have no doubts that

Banshee could destroy one house on a block without damaging any of the others, were it to come to that."

Lockwood waited. Not his call. Not with Lt. General Stoddard here, watching.

They waited.

"We'll see," Stoddard finally granted.

Lockwood nodded.

Probably as good as they could get right now.

He wondered what might change if the CIA started digging up the truth.

CHAPTER 43

Sasha made certain that the door was closed and Ilya was in the hallway keeping watch before he spoke. He and Gennadi had retired to his quarters. Nikon was with Oleg, outside the window.

"Will it work?" Sasha asked, leaving off all the other details.

"You were never intended to be spies against the Americans, Sasha," Gennadi replied. "Merely to go after those men and women who think they have escaped justice. My background might cause you more problems later, but I hope to be able to finesse that with the simple truth that we do not have to be enemies. If they decide that I am unacceptable, my hope is that you can continue to operate with their help. If not, we will make adjustments as we must."

"Someone should tell Kelly that the game has changed again," Sasha offered.

"I am certain that Lockwood will call, as soon as he knows," Gennadi shrugged. "The funniest part about this is that I doubt the Americans knew how badly they had been infiltrated before today. We are not the problem, because I never imagined this sort of situation. Africa or Indochina were more likely."

"Do we continue without you?" Sasha asked.

"Do what is right," Gennadi said. "As always. I selected you, first and foremost, for that. All other things will flow from there. We set out to kill Nazis, but you have saved the world. Possibly a third time now, as I have no doubts that the Americans will start kicking over rocks and discovering far more crawling things than they expected. If Stalin does not have teams in America that can assist an invasion, he is less likely to attempt one."

"I'm more worried about GRU teams able to operate freely in America," Sasha admitted. "I have read about those assassins that Stalin sent after Whites in places like Paris or London. People who had escaped to the West and were living quiet lives, not threatening anyone, but still got killed or abducted and hauled back to prisons or labor camps."

"The true New Soviet Man worries about the weak, Sasha," Gennadi smiled. "Stalin, in perverting that, has proven to be just another Romanov Emperor. Or Marxist Emperor, perhaps. His paranoia and personality will not let him build into the future, because he is always fighting the past."

"And after him?" Sasha asked.

"Whoever it is, Molotov, Khrushchev, or some unknown third, they will be colored by the war," Gennadi turned serious. "By the betrayal of Hitler, after he and Stalin had a neutrality pact."

"Roosevelt was friendly," Sasha remembered. "Trade and a willingness to talk."

"And he is dead, replaced by men like Truman and Churchill," Gennadi said. "That Iron Curtain will remain a thing, because Moscow can only see the threat of Berlin invading them for a third time. Or London and Washington as the *Successor to Empire*. But I must remind you that your mission, like mine, is not a threat to America or Britain. It is, instead, a way to protect them, because if the two great empires can remain at peace long enough, it might become a habit. Neither side is likely to entirely embrace harmony, but perhaps we can keep things calmer, such as they lucked into with the Berlin Airlift."

"Britain will have enough troubles as their empire melts," Sasha nodded. "India, Malaya. How long until Egypt or Hong Kong are gone?"

"Possibly in our lifetime," Gennadi replied. "Britain's pride will force her to struggle against being relegated to a second or perhaps even third tier power. France will be no better, as their African and Indochinese possessions will look around and make demands that cannot be met."

"Will American cease meddling in Latin America?" Sasha asked.

It had started there. Old money aristocracy resistant to allowing their peasant classes any sort of proper liberation.

"I find it unlikely, Sasha," Gennadi said. "If anything, the loss of empires elsewhere will fire up revolutionary movements in Central and South America that force the Americans to fight. Or perhaps to keep invading and overthrowing governments."

"I heard a comment down there that the whole purpose of the US Marine Corps appears to be overthrowing Latin American governments, with pauses for actual wars occasionally."

"And they were not wrong," Gennadi shrugged. "As in Argentina, there is a strong possibility that Lockwood's superiors will hire the Red Branch to assist. And you will, mark my words. You are mercenaries now. Following the dollar wherever it leads."

"South America gets me close to certain people," Sasha smiled cruelly.

Gennadi matched it.

"Just remember that not all of the scientists were Nazis, regardless of what their papers said," Gennadi reminded him. "Tank just wanted to design aircraft, then and now, same as the Horton brothers. Let them. New technology is that future we need, where nobody is remote from the world. Even the Silver Eagle could have been a thing for the betterment of humanity, had they used it to carry people around the world in a day instead of a month."

"The Red Branch will stand between evil and the rest of the world," Sasha stated flatly.

"That, Sasha, is why I hired you."

CHAPTER 44

Lockwood had retired to an office the base commander had assigned to him for exactly these sorts of things, though Ray Stoddard was behind the desk.

Fuming. Drinking whiskey from a highball glass that matched the one in Lockwood's hand. Mid-shelf stuff, but it had been a day.

And tomorrow would be worse, because you could fly a plane cross-country with people if you had to. And he had no doubts that the CIA would be sending at least one team. Maybe a whole, flipping bunch of them.

Soviet infiltrators in Los Angeles? Assassination teams?

"It stinks, Woody," Ray grumbled.

They'd flown together some during the war. Arnold's 8th Air Force. Blue skies and dark nights over Berlin and other places.

"Agreed, Ray, but I'm not certain it changes anything," Lockwood replied. "At least not at our end."

"Are you kidding me?" Ray flared up. "The man's a Soviet spy."

"Ex-spy," Lockwood corrected him. "And he's played pretty straight with me to date, not counting the sorts of evasions and bullshit a man like that might have to spin if he was suddenly in a room with guys like you. Remember, they are Irish by incorporation. South American by work, right up to the point that Sasha and *Banshee* saved Washington. And New York City before that. If this was all some extravagant mission to insert them into Muroc, I gotta tell you that they might be a lot better than us at the espionage game and maybe we should surrender now."

Ray's eyes got ruthless, then he understood and nodded.

"We invited them," Ray finally said. "And it was better that they come here than Texas, because if they were honestly hunting escaped Nazis, I'm pretty sure there would have been a few brawls down there."

"If you don't think Gradskaya couldn't kill a grown man with her bare hands, I got a bridge in Brooklyn to sell you, Ray," Lockwood countered quietly. "But yeah, our Nazis might be people they'd want. I've read about Peenemünde and some of the slave labor shit that went on. And in France, when they were trying to build launch bases for their V-1 and V-2. I'd ask if we were on the wrong side, but Stalin is going to conquer the whole world if nobody stops him."

"Are they really exiles?" Ray asked.

"Seventeen bullet holes in the trucks that we've found so far," Lockwood replied. "Considering a Colt .45, firing into the wind from the back of a moving motorcycle, that's pretty good shooting. I'm amazed none of Sasha's people were hurt, beyond Gennadi bashing his own head."

"Are they too good?" Ray asked.

"Beg pardon?"

"Expert pilots, Woody," Ray said, holding up a finger then

adding more. "Top of the line jets, heavily improved over what the Brits have as a base design. I have looked at the skill set the enlisted cadre bring, and I'm not certain I could find that many holes that they might have as weaknesses."

Lockwood started to reply, then counted.

"Shit, you're right, Ray," he said. "Sniper. Nurse. Demolitions. Mechanical genius. Close combat specialist."

He paused.

"I feel like I need to recruit them a heavy weapons team," Lockwood smiled. "Light mortar or maybe a 1919 Browning machine gun."

"Exactly my point, Woody," Ray nodded. "They are a ground commando that flies. And they have to be damned good there, too, because your *Banshee* has made a lot of our Sabre pilots look junior varsity in the air."

"I'll remind you that she probably has four or eight times as many flight hours as any of them do, Ray," Lockwood said quietly. "Probably way more than you do. They were flying multiple missions a day for years, rather than fifty or seventy-five and home. Hell, I'd recruit her to teach both dogfighting and attack missions if anyone would let me. Same with Sasha or Vanya."

"Can we insert pilots into their organization?" Ray asked.

"Not spies, that much I'm certain about," Lockwood replied. "But Gennadi has a list of folks that have flown Vampires and might be on the market. If Kelly is able to deliver the new Strix, then we have an opening there, especially if they are folks that have flown with the Red Branch here, so maybe bring in a few? And we'll need radar operators, too."

"The new jets are sophisticated enough that one pilot will be able to handle that," Ray growled.

"Kelly thinks that a radar operator will be needed again to

handle a bunch of secondary things, as soon as missiles get smart enough to work at long range," Lockwood replied, holding up a hand as Ray's face got sour. "Yes, I get it. Kelly can be a pain in the ass at times. However, he's almost always right, in my experience, so let's listen to him."

"Guns when everyone else is carrying rockets?" Ray asked sharply.

"Rockets are really only useful, according to theory, if your jet is blasting through an enemy bomber formation at high speed and you just shotgun crap at them," Lockwood offered. "Not worth shit against an enemy fighter in a close range dogfight. Missiles are probably six or eight years from being able to lock on and hit someone evading. And Kelly didn't build an escort fighter. Or a low-level attacker. Or a penetrator. He claims that the Strix will handle all of those tasks pretty well with those new engines Gennadi convinced the Brits to send. Maybe not as well as a single, dedicated platform, but well enough to hand to someone as good as Sasha and let him make it work. If we were facing any sort of major war in the next decade, we might want to build things like it, but right now, it's all in the brush of fading colonial empires, so we have time to keep pushing the margins on technology."

"How did an escaped Soviet spy convince the Brits to sell Kelly engines?" Ray asked. "That's the part I can't figure."

"Me, neither, but he did," Lockwood shrugged. "Maybe licenses to build them coming later, but not my department. You tasked me with evaluating the Red Branch. And Sasha has told us about the new MiG-15 prototypes he flew, so I think the F-86 is well matched, and we'll get better with time and iterations, so I figure we all come out ahead if we ever end up having to fight them directly in something less than an all-out war over Berlin."

"Where?" Ray asked. It was softer than a demand.

"Dunno," Lockwood replied. "Maybe Formosa? Would DC offer the Nationalists F-86 squadrons to protect the place? Would Stalin trust Mao enough to counter with MiGs?"

Ray fell silent. Lockwood watched the man. Known him for a lot of years. He could see the questions nobody could answer.

Or maybe *would* answer.

Lots of potential trust issues, but only at the top. Everything Sasha and *Banshee* had told him had been born out independently by other spies, so they were on the level.

"What does Kryvenko do with a cutting edge jet?" Ray finally asked.

"Keep killing bad people," Lockwood replied evenly. "We can help aim him at a few. Not entirely sure I want to help the British or the French fight their colonial wars, since that's kinda the opposite of 1776, but I'll do what I'm ordered."

"Hunt the Werewolf Legion when we find them?" Ray asked.

"Them and a few others," Lockwood nodded. "Japanese had a thing called Unit 731 during the war that made some of the Nazi death camp people look like an old women's knitting circle. On the day of the surrender, near as we can tell, they executed every single prisoner in all of their camps, then melted into the underbrush and vanished. Don't know that we've ever found the perpetrators or the men who ordered it."

"Sending the Red Branch to China or Asia?" Ray asked, intrigued.

"Actually, I looked and found out that there is a huge subculture of Japanese folks in South America," Lockwood replied. "all along the Pacific Coast of South America as well as Brazil. Immigrants, like they came to California originally.

Good place for bad folks to disappear into if they had bounties on their heads."

Ray cocked his head, obviously surprised, but the man was probably a little too focused on Europe, most of the time.

"And if we get a lead on the gang that attacked them today?" Ray asked.

"Dunno that I'd let *Banshee* fly, but I'm pretty sure Sasha and his people could do one hell of a job on the ground, if someone could convince the cops to keep a perimeter until it was resolved," Lockwood said. "And we probably don't have much time, because that Matveev guy is likely to vanish if he had any smarts. Easy enough to do, if he changed back into civilian clothes and boarded a train somewhere."

Ray nodded sharply.

"Get on the horn and figure out how far he could get, then put a note out to all law enforcement to detain any suspects, motorcycle or train," Ray ordered. "Airports, too. And stir up the police for leads. This suddenly feels like it might evaporate before our eyes if we don't move."

Lockwood heard a dismissal in the man's voice, so he rose.

"Oh, and Woody?" Ray continued. Lockwood paused. "Invoke national security concerns, right up front, so nobody gives you any grief on this one. I'll clear it with the Joint Chiefs."

"*Posse Comitatus*, Ray?" Lockwood asked. Still a felony.

"National emergency, Woody," the general replied. "There are laws on the books right now that allow it. Briefly and for certain purposes. Not that we're likely to violate the Third or Fourth Amendments here, but I'd rather apologize later if I have to."

"I'm on it," Lockwood replied.

And, on the way, he figured that he'd let Sasha know, just in case Ray gave him the go-ahead to unleash the Red Branch.

Even in Southern California.

PART FOUR
CITY OF ANGELS

CHAPTER 45

Kaz had escaped.

So far.

It had taken all day and a good chunk of night to circle around and across the high desert to get to Palmdale, before climbing over the mountains and dropping back down into the basin above Los Angeles.

From there, he had stopped for gasoline and food, unable to hide his riding leathers and hoping that he could instead keep a polite low profile as he traversed the area. Fortunately, there were cafes and gas stations that stayed open exceedingly late, or extremely early, as Los Angeles had many factories building aircraft and other industrial goods, frequently running three shifts in order to supply need.

That meant people on the roads besides him. Restaurants or clubs open, and filled with enough people that he didn't immediately stand out.

Back home, most cities would have closed down and random police officers would likely have stopped him with pointed questions.

Kaz had gotten clear of the ambush without wounds. And

had just barely made it, when two of the trucks had swerved into one another, crushing the first few machines behind him.

There was war, then there was brutality.

Of course, had the team managed to get the trucks to stop, he had been planning to execute Kryvenko and the others by the side of the road, leaving them for the vultures to find. With that in mind, Kaz found that he could not complain overly when someone else rose to the same level of ruthlessness.

He had read parts of the trial transcripts for Kryvenko and Zhidkov. Traitors, all of them, who should be executed for such betrayals.

Kaz looked around the roadside diner where he had eaten and gotten coffee. He was above Los Angeles itself, in an area known as Pasadena. Nice region. Route 66 headed east, though he would not be going all that far.

Still, a single man on a motorcycle at night stood out. And there might be descriptions, at least of the design on his back that had let him fit in with the other to make the attack an act of generic hooliganism, instead of the assassination that it was.

He needed to disappear.

Kaz paid and departed, hoping that nothing about him would cause the middle-aged waitress to contact the authorities. He hopped onto the motorcycle and fired it up, headed east with the small amount of traffic to at least disappear.

The towns along this route were slowly turning into cities. He could see where the entire basin might become a single metroplex in another generation, but for now, there were still dark places where he could hide. Kaz drove sedately and properly, mostly to not give any policeman an excuse to pull him over.

He was still armed, and not about to be taken into custody.

Not tonight.

A few kilometers down the road, he found a nightclub still awake and playing music. Some sort of decadent jazz, heavy with percussion.

It was the full parking lot that drew his eye. Slowing, he pulled into the large space, filled with dozens of dark automobiles, and found a spot away from the front door and bright lights.

Kaz killed his motor and coasted to a stop at the end of a long row, dropping the kickstand and hopping off to walk to a nearby shadow, two nearby buildings coming together at an odd angle to produce an alcove of blackness.

He paused there, dark leathers against dark wall, watching and listening, ready to bolt if he had to.

A motorcycle was fast, but loud and obvious. And not all that common, even in Los Angeles.

He stood out, at a moment when he needed to disappear.

A few folks came and went as he watched. New cars pulling into the lot and circling like sharks until they found a space to park. Others possibly headed home at the end of an evening of dancing and decadence.

An open window on a car not far away drew his eye. American cars frequently had doors that locked, but once you were inside, little prevented you from stealing it.

He needed that tonight.

Kaz waited until there were no strangers walking around and approached. As he got close, a sound drew his ear, but he could not identify it over the music pulsing in the distance. Only when he was close did it resolve.

A man. Asleep in the passenger seat. Snoring.

Kaz almost stepped back to find another victim, when the smell hit him. Bourbon. Lots of it.

He drew his pistol from under his jacket and held it low at his side as he stepped to the open window.

The man was dead drunk. That was the smell. His very pores reeked of alcohol. His snores were heavy and solid, almost like a few Russians Kaz had known. The kind that could not hold their vodka.

He smiled to himself and put his pistol away.

Looking around, he was still alone for the moment, so Kaz opened the passenger door and deftly caught the falling-out drunk, setting the man back upright for the moment so he could strip off the fellow's jacket.

Kaz traded for his leather jacket. It wasn't a great fit, as the man was skinnier, but it would work to disguise him for the moment. He slid his old jacket under a nearby car, then reached in and lifted up the drunk, dragging him backwards with his heels furrowing the dirt, back to that dark notch that had concealed him earlier.

Kaz rested the man there and listened to him snore. Likely no worse for the wear here, as it never rained in southern California in this season. He would awake in the morning, report his car and jacket stolen, and eventually it might be found.

Or not.

The car was merely a tool to get Kaz back to where he had stored all his papers and cash for this mission, hardly expecting everything to blow up in his face so spectacularly.

For that, he owed Kryvenko a slow, painful death. The man had functionally wiped out an entire Spetsnatz team, at a time when there were not that many in place, anywhere in the West.

Kaz had few resources he could call on and trust in this country.

Sliding back to the car, he got in from the passenger side

and confirmed that there weren't any other people asleep in the back before closing the door and moving to the driver's side.

Clutch. Starter. Brake. Gear shifter on the driving column rather than the floor. American. Ford, he thought, but hadn't bothered looking too closely.

Getting it to turn over and purr was reward enough.

Lights. Emergency brake. Reverse gear, slowly backing out while watching all sides for anyone approaching.

Silence outside the window. Darkness.

Kaz got the car into first gear and started forward to the end of the row, then a left across the highway and into what would be the rising sun in many more hours.

He could get to the garage where his other gear was stored, collect it, and then decide to ditch this car or let it carry him away. East to Arizona or south to Mexico?

Something. He needed distance. And heading north again, over either pass, was a foolish idea. By now, the road to Las Vegas or the turnoff to the air base would be filled with angry policemen, looking for other biker criminals that might have escaped.

Kaz had gotten out the front and run counterclockwise over the top, with no idea if Yegorov and Mikhaylov had gotten clear, theirs being the first machine damaged when the ambush had unfolded. Others, he suspected, had not been so lucky, with the few survivors likely wounded and subject to arrest and interrogation, though how quickly someone brought in national police was pure supposition at present.

Evade. Escape. Determine if he had any resources he could call on at present, or if he needed to contact Moscow and possibly fall on his sword for this extravagant failure.

Tomorrow's problem.

Tonight, he drove.

CHAPTER 46

Gennadi had watched the sun go down from an officer's room assigned to him, irritated that he was being left out again. Not too old to fly, but too broken perhaps, with a leg that only usually worked and an arm that would let him hold a coffee mug on a good day.

Today had been a good one. Excellent, even, considering late reports about motorcycles and debris strewn over several kilometers of highway.

And dead men in biker leathers.

Gennadi had no doubts that those men would all turn out to be ciphers when Lockwood's people began digging. Magically appearing out of the fog of war in 1946, with backgrounds that held no more substance than morning dew.

Because he knew exactly how such teams were built. The sudden appearance with believable back stories. The care that went into balancing skills and personalities. The importance of the officers, especially as such men would be operating without backup or communications, save when they got the order to activate for a mission.

Once upon a time, he had studied such plans when

building the Red Branch. Gennadi had simply never expected things to turn out such that he would be actively fighting his own people.

But were they?

Yanina had given him something for the headache, and warned him to not drink any alcohol for several days as he healed, so he had found a cook to brew him a pot of orange coffee. Decaffeinated, at present, because he did not expect that he would be allowed to join the team when they moved again, so he did not need to remain awake all night, like in the war days.

Old and crippled.

It dragged on the soul.

And he had nothing to blunt the pain of betrayal, though Gennadi wasn't entirely certain who had betrayed whom here. His body. His soul. His country. Time, itself?

A knock at the door broke into his reverie. Gennadi answered it, somewhat surprised to find Lockwood Carlyle standing there.

And without any armed guards about to arrest him for... *something*.

Gennadi had also seen the looks those two American generals had exchanged.

"Carlyle," Gennadi nodded.

"Call me Woody," the man replied. "Got a few minutes?"

"I have nothing but time, it seems," Gennadi replied, wondering what mental or social transition had occurred where US Air Force Brigadier General Lockwood Carlyle would allow himself to be called *Woody*. "Come."

He stepped back and gestured to the flat. Bed against one wall. Footlocker slid underneath with his clothes and a single bullet scar from this afternoon. Sasha's Thompson leaned against a nearby chest of drawers, currently clean and with a full magazine inserted, but no bullet in the chamber.

There was a table in the opposite corner, with a small pot of coffee on a strange, electric hotplate. Gennadi pulled out one of the chairs and gestured *Woody* into the other.

"How may I be of service tonight...Woody?" he asked.

"General Stoddard gave me the green light to bring in the full force of the US Government on this one," Woody replied as he took the other mug and poured himself some coffee. "Cops. FBI, including, I think, the team that originally brought Sasha and *Banshee* in. CIA is scrambling, but has resources in LA because of all the airplane factories. Even the Air Force is putting people into it. In short, a major campaign is unfolding as we speak, aimed at tracking down those punks that attacked you this afternoon."

Gennadi nodded. He'd felt the rise of that mad energy earlier. It had hurt all the more for not including him.

"I have been standing here, contemplating how I became such a threat to the Soviet Union that I rated multiple assassination attempts," Gennadi offered. "Though I am willing to impute that to Sasha generally. I am merely Red Branch Command."

"Don't know that I'd shortchange myself, if I were you," Woody nodded, sipping the hot, inky liquid. "You built the team. I've been talking to General Stoddard and we both realized what a great job you did in recruiting."

"Paranoia is a state of being in the Soviet Union," Gennadi shrugged. "I looked around and realized that things were building to another purge, like Stalin did in 1937 when he sought eliminate all traces of Trotsky from the Red Army. Trotsky originally created the institution. Without Zhukov,

Hitler might have won. It was extremely close, and I still suspect that only the weather saved us. Them."

"Them?"

"After today, I am confident that I can never return to the Soviet Union, Woody," Gennadi lied smoothly. Presuming it was a lie. Perhaps. "Even walking down the street in New York City I might encounter a Soviet assassin."

"We've told the FBI and tasked them with looking," Woody said. "At some point, they probably ask to interview you for what you might know about operational procedures of such a thing."

"I will tell them what I can," Gennadi replied, feeling his stomach jolt with cold, even as his heart changed sides.

Changed sides?

If Stalin lacked teams in America—if he could not invade and expect to succeed—would it stay his hand? Or would the next war be atomic bombers flying back and forth to destroy armies and cities?

Europe to the Urals destroyed? Both coasts of America in flames and rubble?

That, Gennadi found firmly, he would not allow. Not after the Red Branch had done so much to save the world.

Inwardly, he wondered if Comrade General Shuysky had foreseen this moment.

Or would forgive him later.

Or if it even mattered.

"You likely to go with Sasha when we find them?" Woody asked.

Gennadi held up his left arm. The damaged one. Flexed his fist, happy that it was working tonight.

There were days when even that was asking too much.

"With this and my leg, I can no longer even fly," Gennadi

grumbled. "Or rather, nothing like combat. Today, I had a machinegun and need, but even then I fired hardly any shots, because I was baiting a trap and Matveev fell into it."

"You did that quite well, from what men on the scene have reported," Woody nodded.

Gennadi shrugged. There was nothing wrong with his brain. Merely the betrayal of his body.

"I have a different question," Woody continued. "Just between us."

Gennadi felt the seriousness of the situation ramp up sharply.

"Go ahead," he said carefully.

"Why only hunt Nazis for gold?" Woody asked. "Lots of other folks have the stuff."

"None of them invaded my homeland," Gennadi replied in a dark, ugly tone. "None of them killed millions of my comrades. Bombed my cities. None of them are *evil*. Or few, at least, and I will reserve the right to go after evil people if I find them. War is hell, but the Nazis were intent on genocide. *Lebensraum* means wiping out all the people in Hitler's way, clear to Vladivostok, so he could recolonize the land with his Aryan *Übermenschen*. Even your Native Americans generally survived, however greatly reduced they were. Hitler would have wiped out the Slavs entirely, and had a great many assistants in the process. The Jews felt it, almost to their extinction, but even Roosevelt would not allow the Jewish people safety when he had the opportunity. Hopefully, they can make something better in Palestine, but I fear that we are witnessing a new empire being born there, and it will continue to be wars for land and water."

Woody nodded, lips pursed.

"So, a gentleman thief, like we encounter in crime books?" he asked.

Gennadi felt his face collapse into confusion.

"A what?"

He sat and listened as Woody explained it. Had more coffee, until he would need a new pot soon. Sounded like a fairy tale, but who was he to comment, after growing up listening to his Babushka talk about Baba Yaga and others?

A man who climbs tall building sides, slips in a window, and acts with ancient chivalry when stealing valuables from the kulaks who had them? Bizarre.

"I might suggest Robin Hood the Englishman as a better fit," Gennadi offered when Woody was done. "Rob from the rich, give to the poor, though in our case, we keep it and use that to fund a fight against evil."

"Yeah, I could see that," Woody agreed. "But I can sell it better, if you are ethical thieves, as far as that goes. Lots of folks will have an issue with your background, but I understand now why you hinted at being White Russian."

"It helped with the British," Gennadi replied. "Churchill might yet return to power, in spite of what Atlee has done to make the world a better place. Safer. Him, I would find problematical on such a topic."

"How did you get them to help?" Woody asked.

Gennadi considered his reply, certain that it would be repeated elsewhere. And possibly used against him.

"Innuendo," he offered finally. "Hints and fragments that let them fill in the wrong pieces to build a picture. From there, it achieved mass and solidity."

"Took advantage of their blind spots, did you?" Woody asked, grinning.

Gennadi shrugged.

"Their sense of fair play is commendable," he replied. "I only exploited it a small amount, as Atlee tried to help the Soviet Union, so there were allies there, while Churchill's people hate Stalin and saw me as a useful foil to exploit in turn. As long as the two sides do not compare notes, none have been the wiser."

Worse? He wasn't lying. But Gennadi also understood that Woody Carlyle could make or break the entire Red Branch project right now if he chose.

A powerful ally that could open many doors, or an implacable foe that would seal them tight.

"What happens if it comes to open war?" Woody turned serious. "Us and the Ruskies?"

Gennadi sipped some coffee and forged his answer with all the care of a new sword on an anvil.

The detonation of a Soviet atom bomb changed many equations, because the Americans could no longer simply bull ahead, solely possessing such power if they chose to destroy Soviet cities and armies in the field indiscriminately. Men like Patton or MacArthur had spoken publicly of starting the next war in order to roll the forces of communism back and annihilate them.

Gennadi found that a lifetime of service under Stalin's abject stupidities had colored the way he saw the world.

The Americans—and even the British—generally believed in freedom to live your own life, though both fell far short in practice and tended to only include white men among such liberties. Africa and Asia were a wakeup call aborning. Liberty from colonization. South America would take longer to get there, mostly because those nations were not American colonies in form. Merely in practice.

But the Americans didn't have labor camps in Siberia. Or

even an equivalent, save for what the southern states did to their black populations. In that, they more resembled Argentina than most European nations.

His sudden, reflexive neutrality took him by surprise. Defending the Soviet position wasn't automatic?

He supposed that he had been seduced by the West, as General Shuysky had warned him of.

Except that it wasn't capitalism or imperialism that had turned his head.

Roosevelt had spoken of Four Freedoms in 1941.

Freedom of Speech. Freedom of Worship. Freedom from Want. But especially, Freedom from Fear.

Gennadi had encountered Addison Walker's ability to print things that would have seen the man imprisoned in Russia. And personally witnessed the destruction of the church and the faithful, but honestly, all Stalin had done was create a new religion to replace them, damning all others as heresy.

Want? He had better coffee in hand that he might have gotten on a Soviet Red Armies Air Base in the best officer's mess. And Sasha had spoken of that first meal on coming to America, a thing so common to an average farmer like John that nobody even mentioned it.

But Freedom from Fear spoke to him now. Nobody had to worry about the NKVD or Ministry of State Security knocking on their door in the middle of the night, arrested for perhaps nothing more than rumors and denunciations spread by an angry neighbor.

More importantly, Roosevelt had spoken of *a world-wide reduction of armaments to such a point and in such a thorough fashion that no nation will be in a position to commit an act of physical aggression against any neighbor—anywhere in the world.*

The goal of an end to war, at a time when Red Armies had conquered every nation east of Berlin, holding them as a defense in depth against a united Germany ever invading again.

And he knew that Stalin would not necessarily stop short of the English Channel, if then. Trotsky had proposed global revolution in his time, but Marx and Engels had expected Communism to arise naturally in Britain or Germany, or even America, an expression of mature industrialism.

Not a backwater peasant nation like Russia. Or China. Both would need generations of development to even achieve the sorts of political and social mores necessary to understand Communism, let along enact it properly.

Had the October Revolution itself been a mistake?

He could feel men in Moscow cry out in sudden pain and rage that he was having these thoughts, but they had chosen to kill him, for the simple act of preventing America from being bombed by rabid Nazi dogs.

And if the Nazis were done for good, would the Iron Curtain divide the world into only two options?

"You've gone exceptionally silent," Woody said quietly.

"Thinking," Gennadi replied automatically. "Your question on war took me places I had not expected."

"Sorry about that."

"No, it is good," Gennadi decided. "Today, circumstances demand that I can defend the Soviet Union or the United States, but not both, so I have to contemplate the entirety of both sides, both the good and the evil each does."

"Evil?"

"Men like von Braun, even as much as they are helping you

today, should have paid the price for what they did," Gennadi said in a voice like a quiet growl. "All of the efforts of Nuremberg, and barely a dozen were convicted for their crimes, instead of hundreds or even thousands who engaged in an evil for the ages? And then the sides fell out and nothing further was done. Berlin became divided. Then isolated, save that somehow your people were able to keep the city alive for a year, even as nobody fired the shot that might have ignited Armageddon. I have no doubts that behind the Red Curtain, terrible things are being done to the innocents of Poland, the Baltics, or the Black Sea states. There are none with clean hands today. Thus, it behooves me to ask: who might bring a better tomorrow?"

Woody leaned back and Gennadi watched the man's eyes flicker back and forth as he did his own calculations.

A mirror, held up to reveal all those things about yourself that perhaps you didn't wish to dwell on.

It pained him, but Gennadi found that he had to lean into the *lesser* evil. An evil, still, but one that contained hope, because Stalin had poisoned everything he touched in his paranoia.

America made promises to the world. It did not always deliver them, but it had stopped the Nazis. And fed prostrate Berlin. The European Recovery Program under General Marshall promised to rebuild Europe, while Stalin wanted all those nations on their knees forever, so that Russia itself was not threatened and any wars would be fought on Polish soil. Even Japan was on the path to becoming a First Rate Power again, though American racism needed to get over itself there.

"The Promise of Hope, as the extension of Roosevelt's Freedom from Fear," Gennadi spoke the words aloud, perhaps damning himself irrevocably.

Or drawing a line in the sand in a place he might never have imagined as recently as a pleasant September day when only America possessed atomic weapons.

"Deep thoughts," Woody replied, equally quiet.

"America can, if it tries, make the world a better place," Gennadi nodded. "Stalin cannot. Molotov or Beria might make it even worse if they were allowed. I cannot speak for the others."

"The Red Branch on a mission to save the world?" Woody asked, eyes both serious and alight with humor.

"Again, Woody. Again," Gennadi smiled. "We've already done it twice."

CHAPTER 47

Sasha had put Yuri in charge of armaments, everyone reloading from crates that had been brought and servicing weapons. He had brought Lyuba and Vanya into his quarters to talk.

"It will not be like the military bases we have struck before, presuming that we find them," he said as they got settled.

"And probably not like Achterberg's palace in Argentina, either," Vanya agreed. "Where would people like that likely live?"

"It was all men," Lyuba noted. "I doubt that they would maintain something like a military barracks. If anything, there is likely to be some sort of warehouse where they gather. Tools to repair their machines and the like. A refrigerator to store cold beer. Each will live individually elsewhere, or perhaps have a larger flat they share with one other. Would it be possible to locate those?"

"Not in the time that we have," Sasha replied. "If there is anything to find, it would be at that warehouse, because tracking them individually to their homes will likely require weeks. The one Gennadi knew will have fled forever by then."

"Is he part of that group?" Vanya asked. "Or sent here to

activate the team? I note that he rode solo, so he did not have a combat wingman that rode behind him. Does that suggest an outsider?"

"It does," Sasha agreed. "Like Gennadi is with us, or will be once we get Pavel properly replaced and are back to teams in the air and on the ground. He might be staying there. Or have stored things there."

"Did he double back later?" Vanya asked.

"No." Lyuba seemed emphatic. "Too much risk. To return, he would have to cross to the west and come over the mountains at Palmdale to be safe. Many hours to get to Los Angeles, then more to complete his circle. And he must be watchful for police with an accurate description. That will slow him down."

"How do we take him?" Vanya asked. "They will not allow us to bomb a neighborhood. Nor can we parachute in."

"We must gather everyone up and drive to Los Angeles," Sasha said. "Now. And position ourselves where we could pounce, if a target is identified."

"Not Los Angeles," Lyuba said. "That's too far west. I seem to remember someone suggesting places near Fontana or Cucamonga, on the roads east towards San Bernardino, were where motorcycle hoodlums were known to congregate. If we presume that they wish to hide among such people, that would be a likely place to look."

"How far?" Sasha asked.

"I believe around one hundred and sixty kilometers driving," Vanya said. "If we left now, two or three hours, depending on traffic."

"Minimal, in the dead of night," Sasha said. "Perhaps we should look into paratrooping at some point, if we need to get somewhere quickly. Lyuba, round everyone up and prepare them to move. Vanya, have Yuri prepare the Camel. He can provide oversight and a way for Lockwood's people to stay in radio contact with us. I will locate General Stoddard and ask him for permission."

"Will he give it?" Vanya asked as they rose.

"Now would be a good time to find out if they intend to deal fairly with us," Sasha replied. "Otherwise, perhaps we need to return to Argentina tomorrow."

He left out any question of if the US Air Force would allow him to leave, in that case.

He would cross that bridge later.

CHAPTER 48

Sasha rapped smartly on the open door but remained in the hallway. Guards had pointed him in this direction, and Lt. General Stoddard looked up from some paperwork in a manila file, his eyes suddenly shrewd as he sat behind a desk.

"Major?" the man asked.

Sasha ignored that part and kept a polite smile on his face. He had grown tired of explaining that he was no longer a test pilot with the Soviet Air Forces, but American officers tended to slot him into that position as a way to place him in a hierarchy.

Perhaps he needed to promote himself to some gaudy and extravagant title at some point, just to make a point? Air Marshall? Sky Commander? *Huntsman General*?

Tomorrow.

"I had a question, an idea, and a request, General," Sasha replied, still outside the threshold.

"Come in. Sit."

Sasha did.

"We have been discussing criminal biker gangs, General," Sasha said. "Someone suggested that they might congregate in a place like Fontana or Cucamonga, which are both several hours away over the pass."

"I'm familiar with those towns," Stoddard nodded. "And a bit of their reputations."

"With your permission, sir, I'd like to stage the Red Branch forward," Sasha said. "Place most of the team on a truck and race madly down to that location, while sending the Camel aloft where Yuri can act in his usual role as Red-Base, providing a communications link to you, or to someone over the mountains when they have a suggestion as to where we might look."

"Now?" Stoddard asked, seemingly surprised.

"Either the man we seek returns to the scene of the crime, as it were, or he flees us, immediately and entirely, and it becomes a task for the FBI and others to perhaps find him later," Sasha replied. "And I fear that we will know the answer to that question by dawn, more likely than not. If the man is as good as Gennadi suggests, we will get one chance at him."

"And you don't want any help?" Stoddard asked pointedly.

"Not tonight, no," Sasha shook his head. "With respect, sir, I know this team. I helped shape them into what they are today. Strangers would be an extra complication, even as I expect that you would send qualified troops to assist. Tomorrow, we can talk about expanding the Red Branch, if you are still interested. That becomes a matter of allowing Kelly to build us more jets than the four or six currently on the line."

Stoddard fell silent and watched him.

"You've done this before," he accused.

"Without explanations, yes," Sasha confirmed. "As Gennadi noted, men who had it coming. In my case, more a case of delayed justice than honorable theft, but making the world a better place."

"Like stealing the Silver Eagle?"

"It was that, or perhaps watch a world war begin in South America, General," Sasha pushed back. "You would not have taken such an attack lightly."

"No, we would not have," Stoddard agreed. Then his eyes changed. "What does your ground team need, if I went looking?"

Sasha leaned back, surprised. Possibly elated, but definitely shocked.

"We have a few gaps identified," he offered. "Gennadi has those details. First and foremost, expert jet pilots who can dogfight at speeds. Low-level attacks are useful. Ability to follow orders without arguing with a bunch of hard-headed Ukrainians."

"I thought you were all Russians." Stoddard seemed surprised, but Sasha supposed that the Soviet Union was always seen in monolithic terms.

"We all used to be Soviet citizens, General," Sasha shrugged. "I was born in Kyiv, in Ukraine, as was Yuri. Many of the others happen to have similar backgrounds. None of us are from Leningrad or Moscow."

"Yuri's the big Cossack?" Stoddard asked.

"And one of my oldest friends in the world," Sasha nodded. "He and I flew missions in Persia to transfer various aircraft from the south up to combat pilots in the north for a good chunk of the war. That gave me a much better understanding of Americans and British later, because those were the people delivering the aircraft to me, frequently."

"I see," Stoddard replied.

Sasha wondered if someone was going to go back to those old wartime files and dig deeper, it they hadn't already. They would find nothing negative.

"And what would you do if we found him for you, Kryvenko?" the General asked after a long beat.

"Take him alive, if possible," Sasha replied. "I have questions, though I doubt that he would willingly provide answers. He would, at least, provide value to you, if there were people the US Government wished to trade for. Other spies, as it were."

"You're not a spy?"

"I am a pilot, General." Sasha let his pique show as he spoke. "And a mercenary who is trying to get rich but will settle for doing the right thing."

"Like saving the world?"

"It is a task that apparently needs doing, General Stoddard," Sasha said coldly. "Will you help me?"

Rude, he supposed, putting the man on the spot, but today had changed all equations about how the Red Branch would operate in the future. For good or ill. Even worse than Stalin's a-bomb.

Stoddard apparently felt it, too.

"What do you need?"

"A truck, a driver, a radio frequency, and whatever luck we can manage," Sasha said, rising and shaking Stoddard's hand as the man did the same.

"I'll see it done," Stoddard said.

"As will I," Sasha agreed.

CHAPTER 49

Kaz drove his stolen car slowly and carefully, unfamiliar with American roads and driving habits. If anything, they tended to be more polite and careful on the road than Moscow's drivers, but nobody here seemed to be in the same sort of mad rush to get somewhere.

And there were also no lanes dedicated for Soviet officials to use, to the exclusion of the rest of the population, or he might have risked one.

He did have to stop and ask directions at one point, mostly because he wasn't certain that he was on the right road. In the territory surrounding Moscow, there were few roads, and they all led inward. Here, things flowed on what he had once heard called a Jeffersonian model, grids precise and square, generally aligned with the compass rose.

Many roads. Many people. Much wealth, much of it frivolously frittered away, from what he had seen over the previous few weeks.

But that wealth had provided Stalin's armies tanks, aircraft, and guns that had let them halt the German advance, then begin crushing it at Kursk. Before grinding it underfoot at Berlin.

Los Angeles had never seen war. Most Americans had no idea what such a thing looked like. Smelled like.

Tasted like.

He drove to the scent of oranges on a still breeze from the southwest, racing inland over the canyons from Santa Ana.

Kaz wondered what this city would look like if it had been subjected to the horrors of Leningrad. Or Stalingrad.

Or Berlin.

Maybe, if he was lucky, he would get to see it someday.

Tonight, he had to get back to base. To retrieve valuable documents that would let him escape this terrible situation, so that he could regroup with the few men left behind for various reasons.

They would have to vanish as well, but those men had such plans prepared. Kaz was the one who needed time and preparations, because this was not his usual operations zone.

Dark streets. Middle of the night, verging over into that time when people were headed home from work or play, while others might be headed to a night shift somewhere, so the roads were busy. And slow.

He took his time, because getting arrested was unacceptable, and killing a policeman attempting it would cause even more troubles later.

But only later.

For now, he had to vanish.

CHAPTER 50

Sasha was the last into the truck, with Lyuba up front, holding a strange map-book she had found or borrowed. He had everyone else aft with him, his Thompson back with Gennadi for now.

If five machineguns were insufficient for the task, then he had stumbled into a major Soviet incursion force and would need to bring in Marines from one of their nearby bases to control the situation.

Or convince Stoddard to let *Banshee* wail.

Tomorrow's problem. Tonight, he had everyone bundled up and holding on as one of their Marine drivers from earlier had won some internal competition to be the one to drive them back over the mountains. He had not asked, confident that it wouldn't make any sense to an outsider anyway.

"Lyuba will place us on the game board," Sasha reminded them over the wind and road sounds.

And the cold. The desert got almost freezing at night, once the sun was long gone. It was almost like being back in Persia, so he had made sure everyone had dressed for it.

"Do we know where we will begin?" Arkadi asked.

"No, and it will only be the opening position," Sasha replied. "Like knights, we will likely cross over and up to threaten our foe, if someone can find them for us. Red-Base will be overhead, so we can communicate, but they are not a weapon we can call on. Everything will be in our hands for now. Lyuba expects a warehouse, so we are likely in an industrial zone of some sort, just off a highway. We are not enough people to hold a perimeter, so we will divide into our two usual teams, with Vanya, Arkadi, and Yanina anchoring a flank and serving as a blocking force, while the rest of us will come in from a back corner to attack, or push them out where someone has a clear shot."

"Are we taking prisoners?" Vanya asked as everyone stirred.

"If possible," Sasha replied, voice going hard. "Most of our weapons fire ball ammunition, which tends to punch through instead of rupturing inside. Once wounded, any foe will likely need medical assistance, so it is not necessary to keep firing, but do not let them threaten you. Call for assistance and the entire team will take them. If we encounter an entire hornet's nest of trouble, use excessive force to contain and stop them."

"Excessive force, commander?" Ilya asked. Team Sergeant. Leader among the others. Spokesman, frequently.

"They intended to assassinate us, Ilya," Sasha reminded him. "Twice. They failed to prepare adequately, but that does not change their intent. Gennadi has a bullet lodged in his footlocker, and plans to leave it there as a permanent reminder of the stakes. I would rather all of you made it home safe, and we had to kill every one of our foes, because they will do the same to us. It has come down to that. Questions?"

He had shocked all of them to silence, but that was to be expected. Many had been recruited for the mission of hunting rogue war criminals, not fellow Soviets.

But the Red Branch had been permanently excised. Exiled. He doubted that the GRU would come to their senses. That Gennadi's superiors would be able to get such assassins called off, because someone would have to leak the truth, and unmask them for what they were.

Except...

What were they?

Not freedom fighters. That would be what those men and women in Asia and Africa called themselves, striving to throw off the colonial yoke.

Mercenaries, yes, but possessed of a higher mission, if the Americans would allow it. Bringing justice for those who had none. Jews. Roma. Homosexuals.

Nobody Sasha knew personally. Nor even cared that much about, save that they were the victims of bullies, and Gennadi had asked him—*tasked the New Soviet Man*—with standing up for such people.

With saving the world.

Keeping a peace, however warm and fragile, between the two faces of the Iron Curtain.

And he would. Perhaps that would be his new calling. It had begun by resisting Nazis. There were others he could thwart as well.

Him, and the Red Branch.

CHAPTER 51

Kaz had approached his base with care, aware that some of the men he had ridden with today had likely been taken alive. They were unlikely to talk, but there would be clues that could lead the police and others to this warehouse. Eventually.

It was unlikely to have occurred this quickly, but it would only take one mistake for him to be cornered. Captured, probably, because he could be traded home later, if the Soviet Union wished to acknowledge him.

Or he could serve prison time without breaking cover, like the man who had assassinated Trotsky in Mexico City, currently a mere murderer in prison.

Whatever the mission required.

He drove past the warehouse, noting that there were lights on, but the same lights from this morning. No activity outside, which was also good.

Kaz had worried that there might already be swarms of police, secret or otherwise, already here and waiting to arrest anyone calling.

Or getting too close.

He kept going on the narrow highway, then turned right two blocks beyond. Off the main road, things got darker, and quieter. Kaz drove on, going down several more blocks before turning inward and coming back. Still looking for whatever trouble might be lurking in those shadows.

He would have one chance when he decided to move, and didn't think that his stolen Ford was up to a car chase to escape the police.

He emerged to the highway again and turned right, back onto the main road. Nothing had stood out. Or moved. Dark buildings, with one all-night diner down almost a kilometer, plus a few neighborhood bars.

His cover with the gang had seen him in the diner and one of the bars at odd hours, but the men had all maintained tight operational security in such places, tough and ready to fight, but minding their manners about it and never throwing the first punch.

No reason for any of them to be arrested. And none had, to date.

Or as recently as yesterday. All of them would be forfeit at some point, those that didn't get away tonight.

This morning. Dawn was still several hours off but coming inexorably. Like the authorities were.

Kaz drove down to the diner and then the bar where his men met. Again, nothing stood out. None of them were out tonight, which was good, as Yegorov had ordered the few of them to gather at the warehouse and await developments.

Like breaking survivors out of a local jail if something went terribly wrong.

Mexico wasn't that far away, if push came to shove. And didn't like Americans all that much, though he wasn't certain how they might react to Soviet infiltrators and provocateurs.

And he'd rather not have to find out.

Kaz found a side street and made his way back to the warehouse, again driving right by it on the backside and seeing nothing that caused him to simply drive away and forget trying to rescue the others.

Mostly satisfied, he found a spot on a curb, down several blocks, and parked the car, leaving the windows down to listen as he shut off the engine.

No sound, other than the night. Cars on the highway a few blocks over. One dog barking, barely audible so some distance away.

Nothing.

He nodded to himself and made sure that the pistol was where he could get to it in a hurry.

Even in an American town, walking around with a gun in your hand was a stupid mistake, silly cowboy movies to the contrary.

He opened the door and slipped out, closing it quietly and standing next to the machine without moving.

Again, no sudden sound. No lights coming on, but he was on a strange street, with houses on the left and the backs of warehouses on the right. The locals were probably used to strange things occurring at three in the morning.

He hoped.

Kaz squared his shoulders and moved to the sidewalk, ambling like a man out for a walk. Never look suspicious, though he had no idea what might qualify in a place like this. Not firm and military. Not skulking.

Somewhere in the middle had to be good enough.

He set off in the direction of the warehouse, keeping his head discreetly on a turret's swivel.

Trouble was out there somewhere.

He had to find it.
And avoid it.

CHAPTER 52

Vanya had the radio in hand, the full team waiting in the back of the truck. Lyuba had gotten them to a place he thought was called Fontana, but wasn't sure.

Semi-industrial, so their truck did not stand out badly. Dark in many places around them, with a lot apparently filled with new cars for sale across the street.

So many unsold vehicles brought home to Vanya how poor his childhood had been. And what strides the West had made in their industrialization, but Russia and the Republics had been mostly agrarian a generation ago. Industry had been located in a few major cities, then quickly broken down and transported by truck or train east of the Urals to protect them from Hitler's savageness.

It would be generations before the Soviet Union caught up with the West. Assuming whoever replaced Stalin succeeded. China was even worse, and two generations behind the Soviet Union.

"Wealth," he murmured.

"Nobody has invaded them," Sasha reminded him. "Not since they invaded and colonized, centuries ago, when it was more like Siberia is today. The other nations intend to catch up with America. If we can keep wars from breaking out, they might."

"Is that our new task?" Vanya asked his commander. "Keeping the peace?"

"A noble one," Sasha replied. "Assuming we can find someone to pay us."

"Would the United Nations participate?" Lyuba asked as she studied her map, not looking up.

"Only if it didn't threaten the important players, I suppose," Sasha told her. "That place is a salon for intellectuals, and not, I think, the prototype of a new world government. But anything is possible, and if the Americans remain involved, it might be more successful than the League of Nations was."

"Strange, moving to such a higher calling," Vanya offered, noticing how the rest of the team had fallen silent from whispers. "But it is the thing we have done. And will continue, once this is complete."

"There is no good excuse for a GRU team to be stationed in California," Sasha said darkly. "None, because they are saboteurs and assassins. That they exist here means that someone intends to use them at some point. That is a crime that must be confronted. A problem that threatens the whole world, so us doing this protects the people around us, even if most of them will never know or understand our efforts."

Vanya started to ask a question when the radio chirped.

"Red-2, this is Red-Base."

"Go ahead, Red-Base," Vanya said, watching the team surge like a bolt of lightning had emerged from the radio, touching all of them.

"You have the map book," Yuri said, then proceeded to list a page and grid number as Lyuba quickly flipped.

It was an interesting thing, this map book. Oversized and spiral bound, to allow someone to see details—ACCURATE details—at close range.

As a commissar, Vanya understood that many Soviet maps were intentionally printed with misleading information, to confuse invading armies and send them the wrong direction. That hadn't worked with Hitler, but there was no way to confuse an army several hundred miles wide as it moved.

"We have the location noted, Red-Base," Vanya said as Lyuba looked up and nodded.

"Known hideout, according to the information relayed to me from up north," Yuri said. "We have moved into a wide orbit at best fuel consumption speed, orbiting clockwise for now and available to relay messages. Proceed to coordinates and investigate."

"In motion, Red-Base," Vanya said. "Not long."

And it wouldn't be, as they were only about ten kilometers away, though the map was printed in miles. Lyuba and Sasha had guessed correctly in placing them by the side of the road.

He watched her exit the bed of the truck by swinging out over space and landing in the open passenger seat.

"Start your engine," she ordered, clear over the quiet night through the open window.

Quickly they were moving.

Would they be in time?

CHAPTER 53

Lyuba had to ride up front, in order to guide the Marine driver, though he knew the general area already, it seemed.

"We can go past it and hit a few places that might be open this late," the young man said earnestly. "Or we can pull short and approach on side streets. Figure the truck stands out. Especially after what we did today."

This man had been driving Vanya, so hadn't damaged his vehicle beyond bullet scars, but obviously saw himself as one of them. She welcomed that attitude, because things had gotten a bit out of hand before.

And likely would again shortly.

"Short and stealthy," Lyuba decided. Sasha had put her in charge of this portion of things. "Come at them from a flank. I will tell you when we are four blocks away and you will find a place to park."

"Aye, aye, sir. Ma'am."

He hunched forward and drove. It helped, her being an officer, as American soldiers had the same hard demarcation between enlisted and officers. And this young man could not compare to Sasha at all, but she wasn't about to tell him that.

Pavel had made that mistake. And paid for it.

Except that she begun to wonder if Pavel had been a double agent planted by someone like the GRU and intended to stop them at the beginning. He had spoken of being seduced by wealth in Argentina, but Lyuba wasn't sure she believed such things, after two more attempts on Sasha's life.

So far.

They roared down the highway for a short time.

"This would be a good place to turn left, coming up," he said.

"Take it," Lyuba replied. "Then in two blocks and right. Pull over after that near the green space."

"By the park. Got it."

They turned, then things got dark on a residential side street. Deeper, they turned and found a park. Or a school yard. It was hard to say, save that she saw swings and other things near a low brick building.

The big truck rolled to a stop and he shut things down.

"You are armed?" Lyuba confirmed.

"Aye, ma'am."

"You will remain in the vehicle, but be prepared to engage anyone fleeing in this direction from our destination," she ordered. "I would presume motorcycles, but they may also be on foot. Do not shoot first. Do not let them get away."

He paused to parse that from the way his face scrunched up, then the young man nodded.

"Got it."

Lyuba nodded back and slid out of the tall vehicle. At the rear, Sasha was first down, with the others rapidly following.

She had left the map book in the cab but had memorized everything she needed with years of experience being able to have an entire map in her head for the next bombing mission.

"This way," she said, turning and cutting into the park and across the grass.

Sasha fell in beside her, and the entire group made remarkably little sound as they moved.

Down two blocks and back one towards the highway, Lyuba found the alley she wanted. She left the others in place and tapped Arkadi Nenashev to join her with his sniper rifle.

"Third block down on the right," she said as they looked around the corner. "The second lit building."

"Stand by," Arkadi murmured, stepping back and bringing his rifle up to quarter the target. "Nobody moving around at present. I'd need to be closer have a high probability of a hit."

"Understood," Lyuba replied. "The blocks run long east to west and short north to south. How close do you need to be?"

"One hundred meters allows Vanya and Yanina to engage with Thompsons," he smiled. "I presume that allows us to seal off an entire flank. I see a couple of bushes on this side of the road that would probably be perfect for that."

"You lead," Lyuba said. "Vanya, you and Yanina with him. I see where he is going. The rest of us will circle around from the highway side to engage."

She looked up at Sasha, standing nearby, and got a quick nod and a flash of a smile from him, so Lyuba crossed the street in this same alley with the team strung out behind her as the others split off.

It helped that the alleys were dark. Packed dirty with gravel, though there were low spots that probably turned into puddles when it rained. Dry now. A bit windy, but not bad. A cat or other small, furry animal that spooked at one point, racing madly away.

Nobody out and about at this time of morning, which was good, because their uniforms would probably raise more questions than they answered. As would a host of machineguns.

She went one block up and looked again. They were on the highway, looking at the fronts of warehouses or factories, so she turned and started towards her target. Another block, and she found a spot where someone had parked a couple of delivery vans, tall and flat-sided in front of a brick building suggesting machine tools or parts. Not aeronautical in nature, so she wasn't sure past that.

"Sasha," she called quietly, drawing him close enough to smell. "There."

"Yes," he replied. "We will give Vanya time to settle in, then we will approach. Nikon, you will have point on the approach, so sling your weapon. Ilya, you will follow close, as I do not have Oleg tonight to bamboozle people with pretty words. Take any innocents down softly if you must use violence."

Lyuba approved.

Quiet, until the moment when noise was needed.

That was coming.

CHAPTER 54

Kaz approached the rear door with care and celerity, knocking three times in rapid sequence, then pausing and knocking three slowly.

A few moments passed before it opened to a man holding a pistol in one hand.

Sgt. Emiliy Petrov. One of the ones left behind for emergencies.

Like this had turned into.

Kaz let the man see his face, then watched him step back and motion.

Kaz entered and the door closed behind him.

"Sir?" Petrov asked.

"The ambush failed," Kaz replied, looking around at the pitiful handful of other men that were all the reserve he had, if he wanted to do something suicidally stupid.

He did not.

"The Red Branch were prepared for us, with machine guns," Kaz continued. "It was a slaughter, out there on the highway to the American air base. I only barely escaped with my life. I presume at this point that any others who have not made it home by now are either dead, in hospitals, or in jail."

They were hard men, all of them. Living this sort of life required it.

He had still shocked them.

"What happened, sir?" Petrov asked, moving back to a table where the men had been seated before, some reading and others playing cards.

They were professionals. And those dead men had been teammates for several years, so Kaz sat down at the table and began his explanation from the point they had watched five trucks roll by.

It took some time to complete, as these men demanded details.

Kaz didn't really have the time to do this, but they deserved the truth. Because as soon as he was able to gather up his own travel gear, they would all have to split up and vanish.

He didn't know what contingency plans the other men had in place, and frankly didn't want to, because the less they all knew about one another going forward, the safer everyone would be.

"From there, I stole a car and parked it a few blocks away, slipping up to the back door here and knocking," Kaz concluded his tale. "I intend to change clothes into something entirely civilian, then walk out to that stolen car and ditch it somewhere else."

Again, he didn't say where. There were options for buses and trains. Even airplanes, if he took a little time.

They would take care of themselves.

All he had needed was the time to get away from them.

"We should activate contingencies?" Petrov asked.

"Not if it involves attacking a jail, no," Kaz countered.

"Disappear now. The others will not be broken immediately, if ever, and you can contact your sources later and get updated orders. I doubt that Los Angeles will be safe for now. Or for some time. You men see to yourselves with Yegorov and Mikhaylov missing in action."

He ignored their comments and rose, moving to where he had a suitcase, spare passports and other papers, and money.

Enough money and misdirection to get back to General Chaykovsky.

Moscow needed to know what had really happened.

And how many much effort it would probably take to destroy the Red Branch, after all.

They had sadly underestimated Aleksandr Kryvenko.

It was not a mistake he would make again.

CHAPTER 55

Vanya had his small binoculars up, mostly as a way to concentrate on a small area as he quartered everything. Yanina being nearby would keep a wider watch, while Arkadi had his scoped rifle focused on the door.

Darkness, lit and broken intermittently, but Arkadi and Lyuba had chosen them a spot with long fields of fire, open without any meaningful cover. He wondered if the people inside had understood that when they chose this as a base.

"Vanya, what about target backstops?" Yanina asked. "This is a residential area on our left, if we turn too far when shooting."

Trust a nurse to consider such things. And she was right.

"The buildings being on the right are brick and will stop bullets nicely," he replied. "I think that you and I should be ready to fire individual bullets for now. We can always shift to fully automatic later if necessary."

She nodded and he heard the click. Vanya went ahead and did the same himself. Arkadi had a bolt-action rifle.

"Arkadi, what is the penetration of that weapon against bricks?" he murmured.

"At close range, I probably penetrate entirely with velocity," he said, never taking his eyes off the back of the target warehouse. "As we get farther away, I will quickly be to a point where they will be tough enough to stop me."

"And an American motorcycle?" Yanina asked.

"Fragile," Arkadi replied. "I believe I killed several of them today, but could not be certain. Some might have been repairable later, but others suffered hits through the fuel tanks and caught fire. Automobiles, however, might be more difficult to damage, because they will be made of a heavy, thick steel. Not armor plate, but this rifle is for killing people."

"Do we need something heavier?" Vanya asked.

"In Leningrad, I know one woman who used a PTRS-41 as a kind of sniper rifle," Arkadi said. "Taking exceptionally long shots, or able to kill tanks that got sideways to her in the rubble. And, of course, Sergeant Yakov Pavlov was made a Hero of the Soviet Union for his actions at Stalingrad, shooting down from rooftops where the top armor of even the heaviest Nazi tanks was thin enough to penetrate."

"Modern tanks will resist on the glacis plate," Vanya mused. "I had not considered that the tops and deck might be thin enough."

"Tankers do not wish to discuss such things," Arkadi chuckled. "The PTRS and PTRD are both enormous weapons, though. Over two meters long. The RD only weighs eighteen kilograms, but it is a bolt action like this, while the RS uses a gas piston."

"Eighteen kilograms?" Vanya confirmed, getting a nod back. "Too big, I suspect, though it probably has its uses. I wonder if you need something more like a big-game rifle instead."

"My Winchester can be scaled up to a .375 H&H

Magnum," Arkadi replied quietly. "African hunters have used that cartridge to take elephants and rhinoceros. Still bolt action. Probably loses some of the excessive range that the .30-06 was intended for, but it would have much greater stopping power at under four hundred meters."

"When we return to base, you and I will have a chat, Arkadi," Vanya decided. "I feel as though our enemies will grow more dangerous, having been bested, and we will need something to surprise them."

"Will they bring armor?" Yanina asked. "Something that will shrug off a small rifle?"

"Who knows," Vanya replied. "It may be that we will need to upgrade Arkadi to something excessive, but I'd rather stick to the ability to kill an average American automobile at a reasonable distance, either fleeing or to ambush them."

"If you have time for an ambush, Ilya will plant explosives," Arkadi said quietly. "Anyone getting out of a damaged tank or scout car is at risk."

"Yes," Vanya agreed. "But we will need to talk to Sasha and perhaps Gennadi, because we have moved on from individual efforts to how we can make the team even more effective. Plus, the Americans are probably serious about offering us pilots and crew to expand the Red Branch."

"What will that mean as teams?" Yanina asked.

"I think that Sasha would shift Ilya and Arkadi to have new pilots initially," Vanya told her. "To train them. You might as well, but Nikon will need a driver, so you are perhaps fourth. Once we have them acclimated to our way of doing things, we might shift around again."

"Would it be useful to begin rotating crews now?" she asked.

Vanya knew that having an all-female flight crew was novel,

but the two were both Night Witches veterans, and had a shorthand he could hardly follow some days.

"Yes, it probably would," he said, seeing where it would initially cause some confusion, but would strengthen the team later. "We will talk to Sasha and see what he thinks."

"Will outsiders fit in?" Arkadi asked delicately.

True outsiders. Folks who did not know the truth about the Red Branch.

Except that they were evolving. Turning into something new. Something better, though they might not be able to hunt their old foes as obviously as before.

Or they might, depending on General Carlyle.

"We will turn them into insiders," Vanya explained. "That will be necessary. And we have space to use them on the ground, as well as in the air."

"Very—hold. I have movement," Arkadi hissed, squaring up on his scope.

Vanya lowered his binoculars to pick up a door that had opened on the back of the factory.

Something was happening.

CHAPTER 56

Kaz moved to the room where he had been sleeping while in California. Not much larger than a closet, but sufficient to keep the noise down when the men were out in the main room.

Off-duty, they were not loud or boisterous, though outsiders would expect it. They worked on their machines. A few had jobs as covers, though the archetype was often seen as a petty criminal by the public.

They had money sufficient to keep them from having to do such things, but did dabble as part of their covers.

As long as he'd been able to sleep, all Kaz had done was make sure that they were ready to move on five minutes warning, which had come three days ago, when the American warship had pulled into port at San Diego with the Red Branch Command aboard and started the process of getting things shipped to the desert.

Quickly, he stripped off the leathers worn over dungarees. Chaps. Vest. The stolen jacket that didn't fit all that well.

Kaz considered what was in the suitcase and decided to abandon most of it. Nothing that would identify him, once he pulled out a small packet containing American, French, and

Canadian passports, all forgeries good enough to work. American Dollars got separated from Francs and Canadian currency, the latter going back into an envelope for now.

Off-the-rack American suit in brown. White shirt. Dark tie. Requisite fedora for his head because Americans were almost classist about their hats. Holster back under his arm where he could get to it quickly. Full magazines for trouble, though he had not been in a position to shoot anything earlier.

Kaz took in the look in his mirror and decided that he could be an accountant or something. Not as flashy as a salesman off on some jaunt. Perhaps brought in to clean up some financial confusion from an office on the East Coast, and now ready to return home.

Anything that let him vanish.

He reached for the door handle and heard a single gunshot ring out, followed by several more.

Trouble, it seems, had found him.

CHAPTER 57

Sasha set himself third, behind Nikon and Ilya and ahead of Lyuba. The three of them had their Thompsons handy, while he left his Shanxi holstered for now. Thinking instead of necessarily shooting, though he could draw and fire quickly. Four should be sufficient if they were prepared.

They emerged from behind the two trucks in a line, moving quickly but not charging. Everyone had a lane to fire into if trouble broke out, and they could lay down a volume of it.

The front of the factory had two big single-bay garage doors side by side, with a smaller door closer. Lights showed through the garage doors, but they were over his head. Letting in daylight, he presumed. The rest of the building was brick. Solid. Dark with a red hue.

He had seen no other doors on the side as they had approached, so Sasha hoped that it might be possible to bottle his foes up. Vanya and his team would have the rear covered, if they had to pin someone down trying to escape that way.

He was not fully confident, but felt that they could do this. Speed in reaction was going to carry them farther than taking the time to scout this and enfilade it properly. The Air Force had invoked some higher authority laws to order the police to withdraw to a distance.

On the highway, traffic had suddenly ceased entirely, a thing he only noticed when the sound dropped to nothing.

"It has begun," he muttered to Lyuba. "They have blocked the highway. Either our foe is inside and hopefully trapped, or outside and will run when he sees what has happened."

She nodded. The others heard.

"Nikon?" he asked.

"Ilya, the door is probably locked," Nikon murmured. "As we did it in Paraguay."

Sasha watched Nikon turn and place his bottom against the wall, looking outwards. Ilya knelt at the lock and studied it. Sasha drew his pistol to cover the man, even as everyone else shifted around.

Ilya fiddled with the lock for a moment, then turned it slowly and smoothly.

"Unlocked," he said, not rising. "Opens inward."

"Commander, lights inside suggest that they are awake," Nikon said. "I will lead. You move to one side. Ilya, you follow, then *Banshee*."

Sasha wished to argue, but they were protecting him. Protecting the Red Branch. And saw themselves as less critical to the mission.

They were wrong, but now was not the time to argue. He nodded and moved to one side, everyone pointing weapons inward.

Nikon turned the lock silently, then shoved it hard, following it in with a rush, his machinegun coming up.

Sasha heard voices raised in alarm. Then gunfire.

CHAPTER 58

Gennadi had followed Woody to the base command post, switching to real coffee because some intelligence agent had come through with an address for Sasha and the others. Not a place he knew, but Gennadi had never really learned that much about America save for a few details one picked up in movies. The Los Angeles and San Francisco of the private detective films. New York City. The Industrial heartland. The endless plains of wheat.

He listened as Woody instructed Yuri. The Red Branch would pounce. Perhaps they would be in time. Everyone was there except Red Branch Command.

As usual.

This was still one of those days when he cursed his broken body, not to be able to be there with them, like he had in Berlin, once upon a time.

The command post was quiet. Local pilots were overhead, flying older propeller aircraft from a base closer to the coast because nobody really had a jet-powered night-fighter today.

Nobody but the Red Branch.

Woody turned away from a quiet conversation with Stoddard and approached, smiling mischievously.

"Got a question," Woody said.

Behind him, Stoddard had a knowing look, so Woody had apparently cleared something with him ahead of time.

"Go on," Gennadi replied.

"I have several Nightvipers on the flight line, prepped and ready," Woody said. "Red-Base is overhead of the target, but not really ready for trouble. You've mentioned your arm and your leg preventing you from dogfighting seriously, but nobody else is up over Los Angeles tonight. Would you be willing to fly combat patrol overhead for Sasha and the others?"

Gennadi stopped himself from scoffing at the stupidity of the suggestion, seeing the seriousness on the two American generals.

They were offering him something special. And both knew it. The ability to fight again, when he had largely settled himself to live behind a desk.

He could not engage in aerial warfare again. Not with any pilot worth their salt.

But he could still fly.

"You will not be in command of the aircraft?" he asked carefully, confirming the offer.

"You are Red Branch Command, Gennadi," Woody said with deadly serious intent. "You should be there."

Gennadi fought back tears that threatened. All he had ever wished was to fly. What little he had been allowed before was enough to keep his skills. And he knew the Nightviper, because he had taken one aloft to test it after some repairs, though he doubted that the others knew that.

Woody understood what the offer meant. Stoddard did, as well.

It was a priceless gift.

"Thank you, Woody," he said. "General Stoddard."

He felt a change take hold. The old pilot who had defeated Alois Voss in the air, at a time when that man might have been the best pilot left in the entire Luftwaffe. Shoulders came down and back. His chin rose. His spine straightened.

Air Force Generals Stoddard and Carlyle both nodded and smiled at the transformation, perhaps seeing in him a mirror of themselves.

"Come," Woody said. "It won't take them long to get in place for their assault."

Gennadi wasn't sure what he could do, with no bombs on the racks of a Nightviper, but he could be there.

It was enough.

CHAPTER 59

Kaz reacted automatically, pistol coming out as he threw open the door, his little closet having no window that he might have otherwise used to escape. The main room at the front of the warehouse was bedlam. Several GRU agents, ducked behind cover, engaging figures by the front door in a firefight.

In blue. And not the US Air Force.

The Red Branch had somehow found him.

For one moment, Kaz almost turned to engage, his rage coming close to overwhelming his sense. Then his training got the better of him and he started to the rear.

One soldier was near the back door. Kaz didn't get a good look at his face to know who. And didn't care.

"Out, you fool," Kaz snapped at the man, even as bullets pecked at the back wall and he had to hunch down if he didn't want to get shot. "There are only two ways out. GO!"

Kaz didn't mention that the first man out the door might get shot when it opened. Let it be someone else. Someone less important than him.

The soldier nodded and rose, moving low as he got to the

rear door, a delivery door on the alley that rolled up like those in front, but not wide enough for most vehicles.

Motorcycles fit perfectly, which was one of the reasons GRU scouts had selected it as a base for the team. Kaz watched the man throw the door open, then slip back to a machine close by. He let the soldier push his motorcycle out into the darkness when nobody opened fire from that direction, following in his wake like a deadly shark in shadows.

Outside, there was almost no cover, so Kaz stayed close to the building, standing in the man's shadows against any snipers choosing to kill him right now.

The soldier hopped onto the machine and jumped to start it, the machine only requiring two tries before it turned over.

The soldier turned back.

"You riding with me, sir?" he asked.

Kaz considered it, then shook his head.

"You go," he ordered. "I have a car a few blocks away that will better fit my disguise."

He waved the man into motion and listened as he foolishly opened his throttle to lay down a screech of burning rubber on the bricks underfoot.

The gunshot was almost masked by the sound of the engine, but Kaz had somehow known it was coming, already doubled over and running for his life as the soldier toppled off the side of the motorcycle like a tree falling majestically in a forest.

Unknown snipers with cover and time to prepare. Kaz had little except speed and fury to carry him as he ran in the man's wake. Not to grab the machine. It would require time to get upright. Merely to zig and zag against someone firing the shot that killed him.

If he could make it to cover, and get lucky that he was running away from his foes instead of right at them, maybe he could survive.

He had nothing to lose at this point.

CHAPTER 60

Sasha followed the others into the room. Large space inside. Those two trucks outside would fix in here easily, perhaps with two more behind them.

It dawned on him that the whole gang that had attacked him yesterday could fit their machines inside here, though there were only a handful at present.

Beyond, tool benches and industrial equipment. Then a spot, clear to the back of the building that had been turned into some sort of break area. That was where the gunfire originated.

Sasha could see several men over there, ducked down or behind things, firing. Nikon had gone to the right. Ilya to the left. Both were firing short bursts with their Thompsons, the sound in here so loud as to be a solid, painful experience. Lyuba had moved behind a motorcycle and was resting her weapon on the seat as she fired.

One of the bikers went over backwards when he was hit. Sasha used the brief lull to move to his right, following Nikon over to where they could crossfire the enemy.

"Out, you fool!" a man's voice yelled from the rear of the space.

Sasha saw one of the men push a motorcycle through a suddenly opened door, then a second followed him.

The others were pinned in place by Ilya and Nikon. One rose to make a break for it and Sasha shot him in the leg, the heavy .45 bullet spinning him in place with a thump that saw the man's pistol flung some distance away.

They didn't have long, but he hoped that Vanya and Arkadi were witnessing the break out the back. Sasha had entered willing to surprise these men and perhaps take them into custody, but they had opened fire immediately and seemed intent on holding the line.

Another started to flee. Ilya's burst propelled him over a motorcycle, the heavy machine toppling on top of the man. One rose from behind a table he had flipped over. Lyuba cut loose with a long burst that pinned the man against the rear wall as it killed him.

That left one, tucked into a corner where he could not be gotten at easily.

And the two that had made it out the rear door.

Now, he would have liked Ilya to have retained a grenade, but they had been more useful yesterday.

"You are alone!" Sasha yelled from his own cover, the shooting having fallen to nothing as abruptly as it had started. "The others are fleeing or dead. You can be arrested if you choose to surrender."

The man's response was a pair of rapid shots, then more silence.

Sasha had been peeking around a pillar. He saw the man turn his Colt sideways, suddenly realizing that he had shot off the magazine.

Sasha lined up a single shot that took the man high in the shoulder. Not necessarily lethal, if he got to a hospital quickly. And didn't do anything that forced one of the others to finish him off.

Ilya surged into motion. Nikon matched him. Lyuba fired a quick burst, but seemed merely intent to keep any heads down.

Sasha was last into motion. And farthest away.

"Two down alive," Ilya called, standing over one with a boot on the man's outstretched arm.

"This one is covered," Nikon said opposite him.

Sasha kept running past both men, pausing at the rear door and listening.

More gunfire, but single shots. Arkadi, it seemed.

"Vanya!" he yelled. "Sasha, coming out."

"He went to your right!" Yanina yelled back, so Sasha turned that way.

Shadows. The gunfire ceased, so Sasha began to jog, glancing back at movement to find Lyuba on his wing.

Like normal.

There. Movement. Down a block, where it drew his eye, so Sasha began to run.

It turned out to be a man opening a car door and throwing himself in. The engine turned over a moment later and gears mashed loudly.

Sasha opened fire. Lyuba joined him. A rear window shattered, but the car raced away on squealing tires.

Sasha got a few more steps and stopped, waving Lyuba to join him.

"Vanya, one sedan, going away!" he yelled back into the darkness. "See if Yuri can somehow track them!"

Then he turned back to see what awaited him in the warehouse.

They had gotten so close, but in his heart Sasha knew that the man he wanted—the one Gennadi had recognized—had been in that car.

And there was no way to stop him escaping.

CHAPTER 61

Kaz hunched low, barely able to see over the steering wheel as he mashed pedals, just barely managing to not hit any parked cars as the rear window exploded inward, the sound like an apocalypse coming for his soul.

But he was clear. Gunfire fell to nothing, but Kaz got to the end of the block and turned before he was willing to sit more upright, aware of at least one sniper in the darkness back there.

Somehow, he had gotten lucky and moved away from them, instead of getting shot in the chest, so Kaz understood that he was living on borrowed time.

And this vehicle would not stand even a cursory inspection by any law enforcement official now, the rear no doubt peppered with bullet holes and the window shot out. He would need to steal something else, and soon, but he needed distance first. Had to get away from the Red Branch before he could activate the next set of contingency plans.

Kaz had papers. Several sets of passports he could use. Money in various currencies he could use once he crossed a border.

If he could get there.

North or south? Mexico was the obvious choice, turning onto the road to San Diego and Tijuana, but that took him right past several major military installations.

North to Canada might surprise his hunters. He could steal a different automobile and drive it along one of several corridors. Or attempt some marathon cross-country insanity that took him into the vicinity of the Great Lakes, where a boat might let him slip into Canada without official notice.

Or even the East Coast.

The options were almost endless, but he had to escape this trap before it closed on his ankle.

The Red Branch had already found him once. And proven to be far more dangerous than any of the briefing materials had expected, so there was something more deadly going on. More than even the Americans assisting, because the Red Branch under the traitor Kryvenko seemed to be operating alone.

Moscow needed to hear these details. He would probably be disgraced, but perhaps he could yet salvage something of all this when the truth came out.

The Red Branch were trouble.

Kaz hit the next intersection and turned left at random, mostly to keep anyone behind him guessing. At the next block, he doubled back, two quick lefts in a row that got him back to the highway.

There was no traffic, but it was four in the morning, and Americans that had left the farm did not need to milk cows or do chores before breakfast, so they tended to sleep in. Factories were the dominant form of civilization in the West. More than the Soviet Union, because they had almost no peasants in this country.

Kaz studied the highway and made a risky but critical decision. If he turned left here, he would keep going away from the warehouse where the ambush had occurred. At the same time, the Red Branch would likely be chasing that direction as soon they could get to whatever vehicles had delivered them.

He turned right. They would be coming at him, but the front of the car was nondescript. No bullet holes that would be obvious to a car coming at him. It was only from the rear that he would stand out.

The diner would be a good place to perhaps steal another car, but he needed to be much farther away from the scene of the crime, as it were, before he attempted something like that.

The police were no doubt watching the vicinity. Or would be, with reports of gunfire in an otherwise quiet neighborhood.

Kaz drew a breath and settled like a good little citizen as he drove. There were no cars in sight, but that did not alarm him.

Away, and he would be safe.

Up ahead, a light in the sky appeared. Above the horizon, but not a star or planet.

Then the front of his car exploded.

CHAPTER 62

Yuri had them in a holding pattern, but had shortened his radius when it became clear that the assault was imminent. Not low enough to be heard easily, and not close, but only a few kilometers out, always looking in.

Junior Sergeant Dmitri Yefimov, a distant cousin to the great war hero, was up front in the navigator's seat. The bomber's station. The Camel could carry bombs, but hardly ever did, generally hauling cargo instead in boxes that hooked to the bomb racks.

"Dmitri, keep an eye out for trouble," Yuri said on the intercom. "We are supposed to be alone up here, but any fool might decide to take off in the early morning without telling anyone."

"Understood, Yuri," Dmitri replied for the nose.

"Red-Base, this is Red-2," Vanya's voice came quietly.

Yuri had turned up the volume, because he had been expecting the ground team to whisper.

"Go ahead," Yuri said.

"The attack has begun," Vanya said. "Gunfire heard. We are—"

The sound of a single shot came through the radio and Yuri winced. It was like someone driving nails into his ears.

"Red-Base, we are engaged," Vanya said in a louder voice. "Descend and go into overwatch immediately."

"Roger that, Red-2," Yuri said. "Closing now."

Yuri had dialed the engines back to the best fuel consumption rate, expecting to be up here for a while, flying his circles. He cut it below that, tasting the edges of stall speed but never getting too close as he banked hard inward and pointed his nose at a spot in the near distance.

The Camel could be an obstreperous beast, but it could also fly amazingly tight circles if he had to.

Like, say, sitting above an enemy base that lacked air defense artillery.

"Dmitri, on the bow," Yuri announced. "Oleg, we will overfly once, then begin close orbiting."

"Do you want the cannons live, Yuri?" Oleg asked from his tailgunner position.

"Negative, Oleg," Yuri replied.

The last thing they needed was to shoot at an American city tonight. Yuri assumed that his job right now was to make sure nobody got away, though an IL-28 was not the aircraft to use when spotting.

Needs must, when the devil drives.

"Red-Base, I have one car fleeing," Vanya said. "Target headed west from two blocks west of the target with headlights on. Track them."

"Dmitri?"

"Come to starboard a shade, Yuri," his navigator replied instantly. "Drop your nose a bit in a shallow dive so I can mark the territory."

Yuri juggled speed, heading, and stall to get Dmitri the

view he wanted. The Camel had a pair of Nudelman-Rikhter NR-23 cannons in the nose. Fixed, unlike the matching pair in a turret aft that Oleg could control.

They were armed.

It would be a terribly desperate situation if someone wanted the Camel to spit on a target.

He could still do it, but Yuri made a note to have a chat with Lyuba later. And possibly to set up some training missions that saw the Camel turned into a low-level attack aircraft.

Who could have predicted that he would need such a thing tonight?

"Yuri, I have him," Dmitri said. "Vanya, your target is seven blocks west and two blocks north of the warehouse. He is about to turn onto the highway. Oleg, we are about to overfly him. Mark the location and tell me when Yuri brings us around."

Yuri nodded and slipped away from his target for a beat, then stood on his other wing to begin another orbit.

"He's turning right," Oleg called. "East. Repeat. EAST!"

That made no sense to Yuri. West got away. East drove right by the warehouse, but he supposed that Sasha might not know the automobile on sight.

"I have him," Dmitri said as they circled back. "Vanya, target is accelerating. Can you intercept?"

"Negative, Red-Base," Vanya replied. "We are in a blocking position rear of the target and the rest of the team is out of contact. Relay your information to Muroc and have them contact the authorities."

Yuri snarled a string of curses under his breath worthy of the smelly beast he flew, but there was nothing he could do right now.

"Yuri, I am picking up another aircraft on radar," Dmitri suddenly called. "Closing at a high rate of speed. Stand by for evasion. Oleg, prepare to defend us."

"Red-Base, this is Red Branch Command," Gennadi's voice was suddenly there. "Approaching your location from the northeast. Where is your target?"

CHAPTER 63

Gennadi jogged as best he could to the flight line, not bothering with a flight suit. The cockpit was pressurized and heated. And they were in Los Angeles, where it never got particularly cold.

Woody had gone ahead, and the ground crew was busy at work when he arrived, so Gennadi was able to climb in and start a rapid preflight. One starter cartridge, and he was sitting atop a purring machine, helmet on, radio keyed, and adrenaline surging to levels he hardly remembered.

It was like his first solo flight. Or standing on the flightline the day after the Nazis had launched Barbarossa and wiped out most of the western air forces on the ground.

His plane had survived, and he'd been one of the few to rise up to face them.

One of the fewer to make it back.

One of only a handful that had seen Berlin fall.

Gennadi had to clench both of his hands into fists and draw a deep breath, nearly overwhelmed with the emotions of the moment.

A glance over and Woody Carlyle nodded from the radar

operator's station. Yes, he understood. Too senior to fly combat anymore, not that there were any wars for the Americans to fight right now, presuming that Stalin now had the means to keep them at bay.

That the Iron Curtain might be a curtain wall holding an American invasion back.

It was an impolite thought, but necessary.

The world was still changing from that day when Hitler had turned east and attacked. And it might be a generation before things settled down into some level of predictable behavior.

"Muroc Tower, this is Red Branch Command," he said after a deep breath to find his voice again. "Requesting clearance to taxi and launch."

The reply nearly overwhelmed him again.

"Red Branch Command, this is Muroc Tower," General Stoddard spoke. "You are cleared to launch. Skies clear to twenty thousand feet. Good luck."

Gennadi pulled everything in as tight as he could hold it, glancing at his left arm and left leg not to betray him tonight.

Then he throttled up and began to roll.

End of the runway. Turn and look northeast over the dry lakebed that made this place so perfect.

A nod, and his Nightviper began to roar.

The craft was like a stallion, racing madly down the concrete strip then vaulting into the night sky.

Gennadi had studied the maps in the control room, so he brought the Nightviper's nose around as he kept climbing. Mountains in the way, but not that terrible to climb over. And time might be crucial, so he kept the throttle wide open, only dialing power back when things began to vibrate.

The American, Yeager, had conquered the sound barrier

from Muroc. Others had gone on and done the same, but nobody really understood that realm yet. And the Nightviper was not configured to achieve it.

Kelly Johnson was building Sasha and the others the craft that would see it done. The Strix. The Night Hunter.

Gennadi swore an oath to himself that he would fly one of them when the squadron arrived. That he would go past the speed of sound itself and look back at the old world.

Perhaps the last time he flew, but perhaps not. He felt reborn as the craft roared into the night sky, so Gennadi understood that he had perhaps previously chosen to settle.

Broken in spirit as much as body, but the warmth of California had changed that.

Maybe he could fly with the Red Branch, instead of merely maintaining their factory base, safe from harm.

Because even Dublin had not been safe from his enemies.

Tonight, Gennadi was looking forward to paying them back.

CHAPTER 64

Gennadi glanced over at Woody's radar screen. They were over the mountains. Low, with a sea of golden lights stretched out to the horizon, it seemed.

One dot, flying low and slow, but the Nightviper was at that same elevation. He was, however, flying much faster, though he took the moment to dial back his velocity, lest he overshoot his target.

"Two miles out," Woody said quietly.

Gennadi nodded, listening to the main radio channel as Red-Base coordinated things from overhead, in his role as team spotter.

"Negative, Red-Base," Red-2 replied to the ongoing conversation. "We are in a blocking position rear of the target and the rest of the team is out of contact. Relay your information to Muroc and have them contact the authorities."

Gennadi nodded. Muroc would be on the telephone with the San Bernardino Sheriff's Office, but that would take time to filter down to a man in a police car.

"Yuri, I am picking up another aircraft on radar," Dmitri

Yefimov barked sharply on the line. "Closing at a high rate of speed. Stand by for evasion. Oleg, prepare to defend us."

"Red-Base, this is Red Branch Command," Gennadi called with a smile in his voice. "Approaching your location from the north east. Where is the target?"

"Gennadi?" Yuri Datsyuk asked, disbelief in his voice.

Another one that thought him too old to fly combat. Gennadi would not begrudge them, as Woody and Stoddard had made it possible tonight.

Had shown him a door Gennadi had forgotten even existed, then stood back as he had kicked it open with his good leg.

"Here," Gennadi said. "Vector me down on your target."

He had checked. All of the Nightviper aircraft were kept armed at all times. It was the easiest way to carry that much ammunition and leaving the magazines empty changed the center of gravity and flight characteristics.

"Command, look for the major east-west highway that runs directly in front of the target address," Dmitri Yefimov called. "One sedan is east bound. The road itself is empty as police had blocked off traffic both directions, but they do not have the manpower available to fully isolate the location, so your target might flee down a side street."

Gennadi nodded and slipped up onto one wing to see the terrain below.

He had flown interceptors during the war, up to and including his beloved La-7, but he also understood how to spot for artillery or bombers trailing.

There.

One car. Driving politely, it seemed.

Gennadi marked the spot, then accelerated away, looping wide and coming in from the east.

Nose on, like that final duel with Voss had begun, two fools jousting in the skies over Berlin.

Gennadi dialed everything back to almost a stall, like he was about to land on this highway. Wires running across it would rip his tail off, but he had no intention of getting that low anyway.

Merely to line up his nose.

A thumb and the firing switch was revealed.

He depressed it and felt the aircraft stutter as he fired a long burst, fighting his bad arm to keep them level and strafing.

Gennadi released the trigger, pulled back, and fed his stallion power, roaring up and reversing quickly before slowing again, like he had just forced another foe to drift past him in combat.

"Red Branch Command, this is Red-Base," Dmitri Yefimov called. "Target has impacted a telephone pole and stopped moving. Repeat, target vehicle is not moving. Ground forces, converge one block west of the warehouse and engage."

"Red-Base, this is Red-2," Vanya replied. "Converging now. Red Branch Command, good shooting."

Gennadi felt his heart swell. Woody offered a hand and he shook it, starting a tight, spiraling climb out and up to altitude.

Four years later, and he could still fly. Perhaps not dogfight, but he could take something in low like the old IL-2 Shturmoviks and wreak havoc.

It was good.

CHAPTER 65

Sasha recognized the sound and began running towards the gunfire. He supposed that not everyone would automatically do the same, but Lyuba stayed close and Vanya's team exploded out of cover to join him.

Around the front, he heard a new sound in the quiet darkness. A car horn, running.

There. Slammed into a pole by the side of the road.

Sasha charged, Shanxi in one hand. Ilya and Nikon had two prisoners under control. And a great many dead men.

Late model Chrysler sedan. Headlights not touching, but pointed at each other where they had wrapped together.

He came around on the street side of the car, noting that someone had chewed the hood to pieces. He was willing to bet on 23mm cannon from the holes.

A man was bent forward over the steering wheel, bleeding from cuts on his face. Sasha smelled smoke and realized that the car was on fire somewhere. Leaking gasoline smell added, so he holstered his pistol, threw open the door, and dragged the man out.

"Get away," he yelled. "It it on fire. Lyuba, get Yanina. I need medical assistance."

"Here, commander," another voice said as he dragged the wounded man across the road and safe.

Yanina took charge. He had some first aid training, but Lyuba hip-checked him out of the way and the two of them went to work, using a canteen to wash away blood.

Sasha stood up to get out of their way. Vanya was immediately at hand.

"Call Muroc and tell them to send police, fire department, and an ambulance immediately," Sasha ordered.

"Already in motion, Sasha," Vanya said. "Gennadi called when he shot the car."

"Gennadi did that?" Sasha stopped cold and turned to face the man.

"Red Branch Command," Vanya grinned. "He's overhead with General Carlyle and Red-Base."

Sasha paused to consider that. And nod, smiling.

The man had been a quiet war hero, fighting the entire war and surviving. Afterwards, doing whatever his superiors asked of him.

It was a feeling Sasha knew well, though he doubted that either of them could have predicted an outcome like this.

Sirens in the distance from both directions, so Sasha simply nodded and stepped out into the road, raising both arms to flag down the approaching emergency vehicles.

They would need to be prepared for what they found when then they started investigating.

A car skidded to a halt nearby and a man in civilian clothes got quickly out.

"Commander Kryvenko?" he asked.

Sasha nodded and began walking that way as a second man emerged.

"Special Agent Thomas, of the FBI, sir," the man said. "This is Special Agent Hollister. Our orders are to place ourselves under your command, sir. What do we need to know?"

Sasha goggled for a moment at that. Lt. General Stoddard or someone had put him in command?

But he supposed that it made sense, as he knew the situation better than anyone just arriving.

"Dead and wounded prisoners that need to be taken into custody," Sasha pointed. "At least three needing a hospital first, as there was an intense firefight inside the warehouse when we arrived. "

"This man might be a Soviet spy," Vanya added.

Vanya was pointing to the driver of the car.

"Soviet?" Thomas asked.

"That's right," Sasha agreed. "You will take charge of the police officers and get the prisoners clear of the building, then lock it down until your own people can investigate it more fully. This is a matter of national security."

Stoddard had told him that those words were a magic incantation he might need to use. It certainly cast a charm on these two FBI agents.

Hollister immediately began barking orders at others arriving and emerging from vehicles. Vanya waved down the fire department and aimed them at the flames licking from under the Chrysler. An ambulance arrived with two black men who got into a brief argument with Yanina before everyone got to work.

Sasha stood off to one side, then waved Thomas to follow him.

The warehouse had not changed. Nikon was standing in the door, with Ilya watching two extremely grumpy men, both wounded.

"Yanina!" he yelled. "Medics here!"

He was not surprised when they sent the two black men from the ambulance to assist.

"Bullet wounds," he told them as they got close. ".45 ball at short range."

"I was with Patton in Europe, sir," the older man nodded. "Seen my share."

"You take charge, then," Sasha said, watching the man flinch. "Both are prisoners, so make sure the FBI or police take them into custody, but I want them alive."

"You got it."

They were gone in a whirlwind of activity that swirled around him, but never seemed to touch.

Sasha let the others flow. They were all experts. And General Stoddard had somehow convinced the FBI that he was in charge, at least until more senior people arrived.

Capturing a GRU Colonel would probably ripple a spasm of energy through the government like an earthquake, but Sasha wasn't a spy. Didn't have to try to maintain two identities, though he had both.

He was a hunter, intent on stopping the Nazis from every returning. And punishing those that might have believed they had gotten away from justice.

And now, he would be a hunted fugitive, if the GRU was after him. And this night would enrage them like few other things.

Hopefully, American Air Forces Generals could protect the Red Branch from future reprisals.

He would need it.

They were committed.

CHAPTER 66

Gennadi had waved off flying today, letting Sasha and the others have the first crack at the brand new aircraft.

He was standing on a walkway outside their hangar, watching as three Strix aircraft came in to land in a triangle formation that required exceptional skill to achieve.

But it was the Red Branch. Lockheed had even taken the time to paint their stag logo onto the tails on both sides. Gennadi approved.

He did not need his cane today, but carrying it had become a habit.

"What do you think?" Kelly Johnson asked, standing beside him in the cool, mid-morning sun as the aircraft came down the long runway and began to taxi.

"Pretty," Gennadi smiled at the man as Johnson started to say something tart, caught himself, and smiled back.

"Pretty sure you could strafe and bomb someone yourself," the man retorted. "Even in Fontana. Got the rails we could attach for drop tanks, bombs, or rockets."

Gennadi nodded.

The CIA, it seemed, had taken personal affront at the

297

entire situation and placed an order for twelve of the craft, modified and upgraded already from the model that had first flown this last summer.

F-90B, they were calling it in their internal documentation.

Sasha and the others simply referred to them as *Strix*. The Night Hunter.

Or possibly The Wild Hunt, depending, since that was a fitting Irish legend that Sasha had leaned into when creating things. Led by *Cernunnos*, Lord of the Hunt.

"I doubt that I will be called upon that often to fly in combat," Gennadi offered evasively.

He had flown a few times since that night. Not combat, because the arm and leg still had moments when they staggered and failed, but fewer.

Perhaps escaping the Moscow cold and the Dublin fog had been necessary for his physical recovery. Capturing GRU Colonel Kazimir Matveev and letting the FBI have him had certainly improved Gennadi's humor.

Though he supposed that there were many GRU Generals in Moscow who wanted him dead. And Comrade General Shuysky could not say anything to anyone.

"Those things fly like a dream," Kelly offered. "All that extra power, and we dialed down a bunch of the mass by cutting the requirement to survive at 12g's. If the penetrator program was going forward, it might be one hell of a competitor, but I've heard the rumors that they're going to cut it entirely and go for...other things."

Gennadi nodded.

Kelly Johnson was a man who knew things. And people.

And could keep his mouth shut.

Gennadi was not offended that Kelly did so now. There were secrets he didn't need to know.

"What's next for the Red Branch?" Kelly asked after the three jets made their way into the hangar and shut down their engines.

Gennadi started walking that way, the younger man falling in to one side.

"Once Sasha and the others are satisfied with the aircraft, we will be traveling to Washington, DC," Gennadi replied. "Meeting with some senior people about possible missions they wish to hire us for. Past that, I have been told little, but I assume that to be a function of the FBI and CIA suddenly uncovering a nest of scorpions in Los Angeles. I have no doubt that there are other such problems, buried in other cities, but that is not the sort of thing that Sasha and his people are geared to hunt. And, I'm sure, a few people still view the entire situation and the company somewhat askance."

"Their mistake," Kelly replied with a grin. "I'm already quietly starting to design the thing that you'll need in five or eight years, assuming that the Red Branch is still in the business."

"Oh?" Gennadi asked, intrigued.

The man was possibly the best aircraft designer alive. **Everyone** agreed on that point.

"Every year since 1943, there has been at least one revolution in jet aviation," Kelly said with deadly earnestness. "I don't see that changing for about five more years, give or take."

"Why?"

"Because the Navy is slow to buy new designs," he said. "They've got their McDonnell F2H Banshees and Grumman F9F Panthers, but both of those are straight-wing aircraft. Low speed stalling concerns, but that keeps them from the top speeds that swept-wing jets can achieve. Gonna bite them in the ass if they get into a fight with Soviet MiGs. Air Force is a little more flexible, but when you are buying hundreds or thousands of aircraft, you have to build full parts chains. And train thousands of pilots. Sasha and the others can move more nimbly, as a result. Smaller air force, but you've gotten funded by the government, and you folks are willing to push the envelope a lot more."

Gennadi agreed. Small, but deadly. Flexible, but capable of being overwhelmed in a major air battle, where there might be hundreds of aircraft at hand.

He had survived a few of those over Poland and Germany.

"Could you build us something carrier-based?" Gennadi pursued, intrigued at the thought of the naval options.

The Soviet Union had never been in a position to build such vessels. Certainly not since such ships had become so dominant in the Pacific War.

"You planning on adding a navy?" Kelly asked, a bit surprised.

"We do not have a base anymore," Gennadi replied. "I do not necessarily wish to depend for everything on the benefice of the US Government."

"Gotcha," Kelly agreed. "Lemme see what I can do. Need powerful engines to offset swept-back wings."

"Could you somehow move the wings around while flying?" Gennadi asked.

Kelly stopped dead and turn to study him.

"Variable geometry?" the man asked in a quiet voice.

"I have no idea," Gennadi replied honestly. "We are dreaming about possible futures. What could you invent?"

"I got about a million ideas, Gennadi," Kelly laughed. "Give me until after Christmas to come up with something."

"We'll need that long to master the Strix, Kelly," Gennadi assured him.

They came around the corner and Gennadi watched the smiles of the entire Red Branch, including the men—and a few women—that had arrived from New York City with Yefim.

What kind of future could they invent?

Gennadi had no idea, but found himself looking forward to it with a smile.

ABOUT THE AUTHOR

Blaze Ward writes science fiction in the Alexandria Station universe (Jessica Keller, The Science Officer, Phil Kosnett, etc.) as well as several other science fiction universes, such as Corsac Fox, Operation Marrakesh, and more. In addition, he is the Editor and Publisher of *Boundary Shock Quarterly Magazine* as well as *Thrill Ride Magazine* . You can find out more at his website www.blazeward.com, as well as Patreon, bluesky, Facebook, Goodreads, and other places.

Blaze's works are available as ebooks, paper, and audio, and can be found at a variety of online vendors. His newsletter comes out regularly, and you can also follow his blog on his website. He really enjoys interacting with fans, and looks forward to any and all questions—even ones about his books!

Never miss a release!
If you'd like to be notified of new releases, sign up for my newsletter.

http://www.blazeward.com/newsletter/

Buy More!
Did you know that you can buy directly from the KRP website?

https://www.knottedroadpress.com/shop/

Connect with Blaze!

Web: www.blazeward.com
Boundary Shock Quarterly (BSQ):
https://www.boundaryshockquarterly.com/

ABOUT KNOTTED ROAD PRESS

Knotted Road Press publishes dynamic fiction set in exotic locations and unique non-fiction voices in genres such as auto-biography, business, cookbooks, and how-to. Our authors cover a wide range of genres including science fiction, fantasy, mystery, literary, and poetry, appealing to all readers. We offer both DRM-free ebooks and print books for a global readership.

Knotted Road Press
www.KnottedRoadPress.com
www.KnottedRoadPress.com/Shop

www.ingramcontent.com/pod-product-compliance
Lightning Source LLC
Chambersburg PA
CBHW060239100726
47907CB00003B/701